Fractions of SANITY

Kristine Elizabeth Wolfe

ISBN: 978-1-7368827-1-9 (Paperback)

Contents

Prologue

She was seventy percent sure that she didn't kill her husband.

How could she? She loved him, didn't she?

She was mostly sure she loved him. At least eighty-five percent. That was a good, very good percentage.

She looked up and stared at the departures list. The monotone voice over the speakers intoned, "Do not leave your baggage unattended. Do not accept articles from unknown persons to carry onto the aircraft. Do not kill your husband."

She looked around in a panic. Did anyone see her?

No, no, no. Her husband was alive. She had no reason to kill him. So, sometimes he came home a little late at night. When she thought about it, he was a very devoted attorney and took very good care of the employees assigned to him. Always willing to pay for dinner (from very nice restaurants!) if they worked late. Yes, his co-workers wore too much perfume, and she could smell it in the air around him like an ever-present halo. Maybe, she would speak to him about that. That much perfume intake couldn't be healthy.

She called him. His voicemail picked up. That was okay. Again, he was just working late. She left a message: "Hi, baby. I just wanted to let you know that I'm going to take a quick trip. To Mexico, I think. I know that it's spur of the moment, but I just feel so stressed right now. I need to unwind. I'm so sorry that I didn't discuss this first. We've just waited so long for a vacation."

She hung up the phone. Did that message make sense? No, it didn't say what she wanted to say.

She called again and received his same voice message extolling her to leave a message and he would call back at his earliest convenience! She responded, "Hi, baby. You know something strange? I called your cellie earlier this afternoon and Jessie answered it. Why would she answer your phone? Where were you? No matter. No matter. Just asking." She finished with a light laugh. She didn't want her husband to think she was worried.

Sixty-five percent sure that she didn't kill her husband.

Looking down, she became aware that she had been methodically rubbing something between her fingers.

Black hair. A lock of it. Her face made an "O" of surprise. My goodness! Didn't that look just like her husband's hair? She examined her fingers. A dry, red substance stained them. Instinctively, she raised her fingers to her face. They were coppery to the smell. She brushed the substance off on her slacks.

Forty-five percent sure that she didn't kill her husband.

Closing her eyes, she tried to remember what had happened before she came here. She went home. She knew that much. Ninety-five percent sure she knew that she went home. Excellent percentage.

Was he home? Yes. Yes, he was home. Seventy-five percent sure he was home.

He was home, but he wasn't alone.

Was he alone? He had to be. Nothing else made sense.

Maybe he wasn't home…maybe she didn't remember correctly.

No, he wasn't home. Seventy-five percent sure he wasn't home. He was working. She was sure of *that*.

Who was home now? Was anybody home?

Something akin to realization niggled at her mind, but she pushed it aside. He obviously wasn't home and no one was at the house right now.

But…how did she have his hair? How?

She cut it. She remembered cutting it with the kitchen scissors. Wait. Did she cut it? Why would she do that? Maybe it was already cut. No, she definitely cut off the lock of hair.

She forty percent remembered cutting it.

Well, she was on her way to Mexico, right? She must have cut it to take a part of him with her—what a lovely reminder of him and of home on her little trip.

She looked around for her luggage and all she could find was her backpack. Had someone stolen her actual baggage? She needed to pay more attention. Everything was fine. She was in control. She approached the ticket counter to purchase a ticket.

The lobby area continued to bustle around her, but showed signs of slowing down and tucking in for the night. She scanned the lobby. There seemed to be fewer people here now than even just five minutes previously.

She approached the counter. She smiled, "Good evening! I just wanted to purchase a ticket to Mexico, please.

A little vacation for myself. My husband and I discussed how it was time for me to relax." She chuckled and shrugged her shoulders in a "What are you going to do?" motion.

The ticket counter lady just stared at her.

She felt her smile falter for a second. She didn't know why because nothing was wrong. Her husband was home asleep or at work. Was he at work? She couldn't remember anymore, but it didn't matter.

Really, it didn't. She was about to go to Mexico. She ninety percent loved her husband. And, when she closed her eyes and really thought about it, she was eighty-five percent sure that she didn't kill him. Never mind that pesky lock of hair. All it amounted to was a bauble.

"Excuse me, can I purchase my ticket?" she asked.

"I...I...I, oh god," the ticket counter lady stammered.

"What?" She was getting cross now. She thought, "Customer service has completely been on such a decline lately."

"Television. You...TV...news...searching."

"What are you talking about?" She was beginning to worry. That small niggle in her brain became more persistent.

Ticket Counter Lady began to back away and started screaming and pointing.

She rolled her eyes, "Well...there is no need for this. I can just go to a different airline."

She looked to the side and saw police officers running through the center of the lobby. She watched as a child was accidentally pushed and fell comically to the floor. She could count the candies that spilled from his chubby hand.

She yelled, "What IS happening? What IS the MATTER? I know I ninety-five percent love my husband!

I love him. I love him." She held up her bloody trinket as proof. "See! This! This is what love looks like!"

She felt herself being shoved to the ground. She still didn't understand what was happening. After all, she was one hundred percent sure she didn't kill her husband. One hundred percent sure.

And, almost nothing in this world was one hundred percent sure.

Chapter One

Alice

ohn! John! I'm leaving for work now! I'm running behind! I poured a glass of juice for you, but I accidentally knocked it over. So sorry! No more juice left in the fridge. I will try to remember to pick some more up tonight at the grocery store." Alice Smith called out to her husband as she ran out the door.

Alice slammed the front door and stutter-stepped towards her car in the way women do when they wear heels and try to move quickly. She reached into her purse for her keys and promptly dropped them on the ground. "Dang it!"

"Alice! Alice! You forgot your laptop by the door!" John stuck his head out of the house and yelled.

"I put it there so I wouldn't forget it," she informed him.

John jogged down the porch steps and handed her the laptop, kissing her absently on the cheek. "You're going to be great today," he promised.

Alice smiled at her husband and jumped into the car. She checked both side mirrors and her rearview before she backed out of the driveway. Her drive to work would take approximately twelve minutes and she was already one minute behind.

She mentally reviewed her workday as she came to a full and complete stop at the stop sign. She had a meeting at ten o'clock with the life insurance department. She had been inputting data into her computer for the last six months to try and see if there was any statistical correlation between food security and diabetes management in vulnerable populations. Specifically, vulnerable populations living in a food desert or without access to a personal physician within a fifteen-minute radius. Her presentation would show a very high correlation between the two which would reflect in the life insurance premiums issued from the company.

Because she was running fifty-four seconds late, her regular parking spot was taken. She parked a few spots down, but internally added another thirty-two seconds before she reached her desk. Groaning inwardly, she made her way to the elevator as quickly as possible.

"Hold the elevator!" She looked over to see Ryan jogging to catch her. She smiled and held it, even though this would add even more time to her already disrupted schedule. He wore a blue Hawaiian shirt with parrots sprinkled throughout. His short blonde hair was artfully messy. Instinctively, Alice touched her hair to see if it was in order. It wasn't.

When he caught up to her, he panted, "And, how are we doing, lovely Alice?"

"Running late as always," she responded while trying to tame her frizzy locks.

"It doesn't count as late until you are fifteen minutes late at least. Your hair is fine, sweetness, but you do know that you have a run in your stockings?"

Alice looked down, "Poop! Poop! Poop!"

Ryan raised his brows, "Language, please."

"I just have that big meeting and I forgot to put another pair of pantyhose into my desk after I used the last ones. I'm such a mess. All I can think about is this presentation. While it has been absolutely fascinating, I can't seem to focus on anything else. Do you know I accidentally dumped John's orange juice this morning? I didn't wait to see how he responds about the spill, but I'm sure he's not happy. He already had to bring me my laptop because I forgot it." Alice pursed her lips and sighed.

"I'm sure he can pour his own orange juice."

"What if I also said I didn't clean up the one that I spilled because I was in such a rush?"

"That's going to be more of a problem. No one wants to clean up someone else's mess."

"No man, you mean," Alice corrected.

"No. I mean no person. It's just rude."

"I poured it for him in the first place! I was being nice."

"If John had to clean it up, you aren't getting any brownie points."

"Ryan, I seriously don't need to take relationship advice from you. How long were you in your last relationship? Three weeks and two days? Marriage is give and take. John and I have been together for ten years and three months. He understands I was trying to do something nice."

"Mmm...hmmm."

"Anyway, speaking of doing something nice. Have you been able to get in touch with Natalie? I haven't heard from her," Alice inquired.

Natalie McInroe worked with Alice and Ryan at the insurance firm. She used to complete their threesome which made up the Three Insurance Musketeers. Alice thought Natalie had taken unpaid leave for an undisclosed amount of time. But when Alice checked Natalie's office earlier in the week, the office had been completely cleared of Natalie's things.

"I heard she lost her job," Ryan answered.

"Lost her job? For what?"

"Some scandalously unknown scandal."

"A scandalously unknown scandal? I'm buying you a thesaurus for Christmas. Listening to you talk hurts my feelings."

Ryan playfully punched Alice in the arm. "Aw, come on. How often do you get to use the word scandal? Besides, you know I'm Jewish."

"Hanukkah, then. You use the word scandal approximately eight times a day," Alice replied. "Have you spoken to her?"

"Not yet. She's avoiding me, but you know that I'll track her down eventually," Ryan proclaimed.

"Ok. When you do, let me know what's going on. All of this mystery is not like her."

"I know. It's all part of a scandalously unknown scandal."

Alice just shook her head.

Ryan laughed. "Get out of here! You are going to be amazing at your presentation. I can't wait to hear about how fabulous you were. I'm sure it will be the talk of the water cooler this afternoon."

*   *   *

Alice arrived at her ten-foot by ten-foot office and promptly tripped over a stack of books she had put aside to use for research. She fell into her desk and bent her right wrist back. She cradled the hurt appendage in her left hand for thirty-eight seconds before taking a deep breath. She began to search through said desk hoping for a spare set of pantyhose. She found a birthday card for her mother that she had thought she had mailed three weeks ago; a pack of gum that appeared to be five years old; the earring she lost a month ago; but, no pantyhose.

She sighed and realized she would go into her big meeting looking slightly dumpy. It wasn't just the run in her hose. She needed a haircut. Her curly hair was starting to frizz with the summer humidity. She never wore makeup, and she felt the crow's-feet starting to become more prominent around her eyes. Her personal shopper was on maternity leave. The woman who took her place had seemed to understand Alice's preferences and the appropriate size for her small frame. However, when the suit arrived the sleeves hung way too long, and the shoulders would have better fit a linebacker as opposed to a five-foot three-inch woman. She would have to send it in to be tailored. She was only wearing it because it was the only one currently clean. She still needed to drop off her own and John's suits at the dry cleaner's.

Pulling her laptop out of the case, she began to review her work. She had been over this presentation approximately 643 times this weekend. She needed it to be perfect. A thirty percent probability existed that she would still forget something when she reviewed it for the board. John made her set aside two extra anxiety pills. "Just in case you need them," he assured her. "Your presentation should be fine."

She clicked through her first three slides, which gave a general overview of the difference between Type I and Type II diabetes. After that, she would discuss the characteristics of the population she had been studying to include the effects of food insecurity. Next, she would brief the room on the statistics overlapping between the two areas.

Satisfied that she knew her presentation, she checked her handouts one more time. Taking a meditative breath, she headed towards the conference room.

She was the first one in the room which is the way she liked it. She placed a copy of each of the handouts on the table in front of every empty seat. Once everyone had shuffled in, she turned to face them and smiled, "My name is Alice Smith, and I am so excited to brief you on my research today...."

Chapter Two

Jessica

She was not a beautiful woman. Certainly, not an ugly woman. She was 5'9", 150 pounds, honey-colored shoulder-length hair, and brown eyes light enough to match her hair. She sat with her back straight in the office chair typing up the latest court pleadings for her current boss, John Smith. Both high-heeled feet set perfectly on the ground to facilitate faster typing. Her pencil skirt skimmed the tops of her thighs with her blouse open one button more than actually necessary.

She was an extremely competent woman. Competency has its own kind of beauty, but generally not the type of beauty a man notices outside of an office setting. But in an office setting with very little other competition, even ordinary women could become beautiful.

When she felt Mr. Smith starting to take an interest, she wasn't surprised. He would sometimes bring her coffee and sit for a while to chat. Or, make up excuses to come and talk to her. It was a little cliché, really. She was his paralegal. It seemed to Jessica that this was the way that relationships started now. Her last relationship had also been with her male employer. It was a reflection on men not wanting to try too hard to find a significant other.

Mr. Smith's wife consistently called him to ask for mundane assurances regarding her work or her appearance. Sometimes, she just called because she had forgotten to pick up her medication. Or, she would call because a prank call spooked her. Jessica would watch Mr. Smith patiently take those calls. He would roll his eyes to show Jessica the unimportance of these latest "problems."

She enjoyed Mr. Smith's attention, and she was waiting for him to take the next step. Jessica had played this game enough times to know that this dance required exact rhythm and a perfect crescendo before the finale.

"Hey, Jessie. How are you today?"

"I'm great, Mr. Smith. How are you?"

"How many times do I have to ask you to call me John?"

"Likely a few more times as it is my job to call you Mr. Smith."

"I see. I just feel like I can talk to you. Differently, than I can talk to my wife. I hope that doesn't upset you. Do you know what she did today? Right before I had to leave to come into the office?"

"No, sir, I don't know."

"She spilled orange juice all over the counter and let it drip onto the floor. I literally had to mop the kitchen before I could walk out the door. She can be so frustrating and a complete ditz."

"I'm sorry, sir."

"I can't tell you how nice it is to come into the office and have everything in order. It means a lot that you put so much effort into making my life easier," Mr. Smith complimented her.

She was his fourth paralegal in the last two years. She had not been told why the previous women had left the office. She certainly was not different from anyone who came before her. She could see the competency in the files that she took over.

"I love my wife, though. I don't want you to think that I don't."

"Mr. Smith, I have never implied that you didn't love your wife, and that certainly doesn't matter to me. Is there something I can do for you right now?"

He looked at her. "I think I need to work late tonight. Would you be able to stay in the office and help me? This new case is going to take an extra amount of time. I will make sure that we have some dinner."

Jessica tilted her head. She understood the real question that lay behind the words. Men always meant the same thing because they were predictable creatures. "John, I am available whenever you need me."

﹡   ﹡   ﹡

Later that day, Jessica continued to look for cases through LexisNexis, a legal research site, for John regarding his upcoming criminal defense trial. The criminal cases were Jessica's favorites. She enjoyed helping to point out police mistakes. For this particular one, the police had entered the defendant's home with a "no-knock" warrant. John wanted to allege that the warrant on its face was obviously invalid, due to it being overly broad and general.

A curvy brunette walked into the office. Very pretty in an obvious way. The brunette said, "Hi. My name is Natalie McInroe. I have an appointment with John Smith at two o'clock."

Jessica glanced up at the wall clock. It was five till. "We ask our clients to come twenty minutes prior so they can fill out the initial intake information. Here's a sheet. Fill it out quickly, please."

"I'm not a client," the woman stated. "I don't need to fill out this sheet."

"You need to fill it out if you expect to see Mr. Smith."

"Would you just page him and tell him that I'm here?" the woman asked.

"No. I'm sorry. Mr. Smith is an important man," Jessica eyed the woman. "If you don't have time to fill out the form, I would be happy to reschedule for you."

The woman snatched the paperwork from Jessica. "I'll fill it out. Just tell John that I'm here."

Jessica picked up the phone and dialed John's office extension. "Your two o'clock is here."

"My two o'clock?"

"A Natalie McInroe? She claims to have an appointment, but I don't see it in the book."

"Send her back," John said.

"She hasn't finished the intake paperwork," Jessica responded.

"I don't care. Send her back. I just want to get this over with."

Jessica stared hard at the woman before she stated, "Ma'am, Mr. Smith is ready for you."

"Of course, he is." The woman threw the unfinished paperwork at Jessica. It landed on her desk. The woman hadn't made a particularly good attempt to finish it. Only the name blank had been filled out.

Twenty minutes later, the woman left. Her eyes were red and damp with mascara tracks down her face. She slammed the door on her way out.

"Mr. Smith, I don't have a code for your time. Which client do I need to bill?"

"Don't bill anyone. This was my personal time. Please forget that woman was ever here."

"Already done, Mr. Smith."

Jessica click-clacked on her computer. She pulled up the name Natalie McInroe in the case management system. Spelled the same as the half-finished intake form. The only entry coming showed a divorce/custody agreement in the system. Ms. McInroe had been married to Stephen McInroe, one of the law firm partners. The husband now sought to terminate the marriage and receive full custody of two young children. The documents did not list a new address. Nor was a service date recorded indicating Natalie McInroe had received the divorce paperwork.

Chapter Three

Natalie

Natalie McInroe entered the posh office about five minutes before two o'clock. She lied to the receptionist serving as the gatekeeper at the front desk and claimed to have an appointment with John at two. The receptionist handed her some paperwork and called John.

He immediately asked for her to come back to his office and she was spared any more conversation with the uptight blonde. Natalie's head pounded and her palms began to sweat as she walked back into John's office.

John stood up. "Natalie, I can't say I'm happy to see you. What if someone sees you?"

"Well, if you would answer my calls, I wouldn't have to do it this way."

"Did anyone see you? Did your husband see you?"

"I don't know. I really don't. I tried to be careful, but…," Natalie shrugged.

John sighed, "This is going to be fodder for gossip."

"You didn't think there was going to be gossip before or did you just not care?"

"Ok. Ok. I don't want to fight. What do you want?"

"When my husband finds out about this, he's going to divorce me."

"What makes you think he doesn't already know? He's not a stupid man. Surely, he's watched you become all doe-eyed around me. You can't help it. You act like a silly schoolgirl."

"Don't flatter yourself. He hasn't said anything. He doesn't know. He would have said something." She repeated softly, "He would have said something."

"My dear. I guarantee he knows. Do you know how I know? Because he's asked a Junior Associate to draft divorce papers and those papers have been entered into the firm's case management system. I saw the papers myself. I have to admit, I was a little curious about the details. You're going to lose your kids. Salacious stuff," John said.

Natalie sat down hard on the office chair and put her face in her hands. She whispered, "He already knows."

"I hope you have extra money in your panties' drawer. He'll try to freeze your assets next. You should get a good attorney, because your husband retained a great firm," John offered.

"What am I supposed to do?"

"That's not my problem. Which gets around to the question I originally asked, what exactly are you doing here?"

"I need help."

"I am the last person you should be asking for help. Because I am the last person who cares."

"You should care. You should care a lot. You did this to me. You put me in this position. Does Alice know? Does Alice know what we did?"

"If memory serves, you were a willing participant. I thought what we were doing was clear from the beginning. I would take care of my marriage and you would take care of yours. Alice doesn't know. It looks like you didn't do a good job holding up your end of the bargain. My marriage is fine," John sneered. "Besides, what kind of help do you want from me?"

"Do you think you could talk to my husband? Do you think you could tell him that the affair didn't mean anything?"

"An affair? What we had wasn't important enough to have a name," John said. "Alice and I don't talk to your husband anymore. We stopped hanging out with him after you decided to break off our little understanding."

"I couldn't do it anymore! I couldn't lie to him! It was killing me. I thought you and I had something special. I can't believe that you don't care about me at all. I thought we had a connection."

"My intentions were incredibly clear from the beginning. I guess everything is fun and games until someone loses an eye...or a marriage. You are the one who is confused. You are the one losing your marriage. You took those actions. You deserve what you get. I can't help you, Natalie. Figure it out on your own. You're a big girl, now."

"What if he kicks me out of the house? What am I supposed to do then?"

"I hate it when women expect to get paid for their efforts in bed," John said, making Natalie flinch.

"Whatever. If you can no longer live in your home due to circumstances brought about by your own actions, I'll help find you an apartment," John offered primly.

"I might need money."

"We'll talk about that when the time comes."

"I'll tell Alice. I swear I will."

"Aw…tattling. Always the loser's last resort."

"I promise I'll tell Alice."

"Explain to me exactly what you would say. You would have to say it to her face, you know. What would you say? I've been having sex with your husband," he paused. "Have you kept track of how many times? She might be interested." John looked genuinely curious.

Natalie shook her head.

"Get out of here, Natalie. Don't show up again. I actually have real work to get done. Let me know if you need that apartment," John dismissed her.

Natalie wrapped her arms around herself and walked out of the office. She held her head down so that no one could see her face.

Driving home, Natalie considered the situation. The thought of telling Alice what she had done made her sick in the pit of her stomach. But, John couldn't get away with treating Natalie like an animal. Like someone who had no importance.

There should be consequences.

There needed to be consequences.

Chapter Four

Alice

"Hey babe, I'm working late tonight. Don't worry about dinner. I'll just pick something up at the office. Also, Aruba." Alice listened to her husband's voicemail and did a little jig. She hadn't been looking forward to making dinner tonight. She just felt drained and wanted nothing more than a baked potato for dinner and a little reality TV. She hadn't been looking forward to entertaining John tonight. Sometimes, a woman needed a little solitude and a glass of wine.

Lately, John had worked late increasingly often. Sometimes three or four nights a week. He was on the partner track at his law firm, which meant more billable hours than could be tracked in a traditional nine to five workday. When he made partner, they were going to go on a vacation. Alice hoped for a very long vacation to an exotic location. Their inside joke was to sign off and say goodbye using their next vacation destination.

Alice had met John in a coffee shop at college. She was studying for her advanced economics test and waiting in line to purchase an espresso. When it was her turn to pay, she realized she had forgotten her wallet at home. All very handsome and very gallant, John said, "May I?" He paid for her coffee. The next day, he paid for her coffee again. And, the next. He bought her coffee every day for a month before he asked for her permission to take her to dinner. They dated for a year before he proposed. Their wedding was splashed across the local society page of the paper. Alice's father spent three hundred thousand dollars to make her wedding perfect. This amount accounted for thirty percent of her father's previous year's income, which was a respectable amount to spend on a society wedding.

Alice still smiled when she remembered the wedding. Two hundred and seven of their closest friends watched her walk down the aisle in a white Vera Wang dress cut to lengthen her silhouette. Her train followed after her in dramatic fashion. She could still smell the roses in her bouquet. And, John. John stood at the end of the aisle wearing a perfect suit. Looking extraordinarily handsome with his dark, Mediterranean looks.

Alice dialed John's number. She said, "Hey. I just wanted to check in with you before I settled in for the night."

John answered, "Good. I was worried that I wouldn't be able to chat with you today. How was the big meeting?"

"It went long, but ultimately well. They are going to increase the coefficient for the premiums. Everyone was pleased with my research and it's going to make the number crunchers happy to be able to charge more money." Alice stopped herself in the middle of her explanation, remembering too late that John didn't like her to go on at length about her job.

She knew that she had a dull job. She spent the bulk of her existence looking at numbers. Figuring out how these numbers co-existed with those numbers. She couldn't blame John for not showing more interest in her career. Most people wouldn't be interested in her daily routine or her daily tasks. Just because they were married didn't mean John had to care about her work. She needed to remember to be mindful of other people's feelings.

"That sounds like a fascinating meeting." Alice felt the boredom in his voice. His tone became school marmish as he continued, "Also, I cleaned up the orange juice you spilled. It would have been nice if you had wiped it up off the counter."

Alice could hear his eyes roll. "I remembered that I wanted to make you breakfast, but I was super late. I settled on pouring juice, so I could at least do something nice for you. It spilled just as I was running out the door. I was super late for work. I will try to be more graceful in the future like a prima donna ballerina. I'll raise my arms and do a pirouette while magically pouring the perfect glass of juice and dance my way out the door."

"Thank you for at least thinking of me this morning, but we both know that your magical gracefulness isn't going to happen, my Queen Klutz," John chuckled. "I have to get back to work. I'm glad that we could chat for a second. I will be stealthy quiet when I get home tonight. It's going to be a late one."

"Big case?"

"You have no idea. This one ended up in the papers and the partners keep checking on it every day. They are driving me insane. Natalie's husband keeps dropping by as well."

"Does…" Alice started.

John interrupted, "Before you ask, we don't talk about her."

"If you find an opening to ask about her, please do," Alice paused. "Be home soon. I miss you. Let me know if there's any way that I can help you. I'm always willing to listen to your arguments about a case. I can counter-argue with the best of them." She punched the air to illustrate her point to no one.

"I know, sweetheart. But, I think Jessie and I are just going to have to stay late and work through this thing."

"Is that your new paralegal? Jessie? Does she like it when you call her Jessie?" Alice asked, inwardly knowing the answer.

"Meh. She's never complained. You know how these girls are. I just need them to take diction and draft a few complaints. Besides, it's quicker to say. She likely won't be around that long. I don't seem to have any luck with new hires lately."

Alice heard a female voice in the background, "John, how do you want me to organize these notes?"

"Gotta go. Work calls. I love you. Talk to you later. Think about the Maldives."

"Galapagos Islands," Alice replied.

*   *   *

With her wifely duties accomplished, Alice cued up the latest episode of Survivor and threw her baked potato in the oven. It always tasted creamier in the oven, even though it could take up to eighty-five minutes longer than in the microwave. She prepared the toppings: thirty-five percent cheese, thirty percent bacon, twenty percent sour cream, fifteen percent chives. A perfect potato.

As she sat down, she wondered about the voice she heard in the background. Jessie, John said. John was having a horrible time trying to find a good assistant. This must be the fourth or fifth one in the last few years. Hopefully, this one would stick around for a while. It didn't help that John insisted on calling them his girls. Alice would talk to him about that little habit. Alice needed him to have a paralegal that would help manage his stress.

Alice glanced at the clock. 6:30 p.m. She would watch TV for sixty more minutes and wait for dinner. Thirty minutes for her to enjoy dinner. Then, wipe down the countertops in the kitchen which would take approximately two minutes. At 8:02 p.m., she would read her book for fifty-eight minutes and be asleep by 9:04.

The house phone rang. For whatever reason that John couldn't articulate, they still had a landline. And it was the oldest phone known to man. Probably created around 4 B.C. No caller ID. Alice considered it a colossal waste of money in an era when everyone had cell phones. But, divorces hinge on the battles picked in a marriage, and this wasn't a battle worth fighting.

She answered the call. "Hello? This is Alice."

Nothing on the other end.

"Hello-o. This is Alice."

Still nothing. "Hello? Hello? Anyone there?"

They had been receiving prank calls on the landline lately. She would pick up the phone and there would be nothing on the other end. When John answered the phone, there seemed to be some talk back and forth. John never discussed them, because he didn't want her to worry. She had begged John to report the calls, but he shrugged them off. She asked him to at least change their phone number, but he wouldn't agree to that either. The only time he agreed to file a report was when someone threw a rock through the window. When the person wasn't caught, he constantly used that excuse not to bother with the police. Because, according to John, the police wouldn't do anything about them anyway.

She tried to respond light-heartedly. "Well, if this is a prank call. It isn't very good. You need to think of something interesting to say. Like I'm looking for Al. Last name Coholic. That would be funny and worth answering the phone for."

"Your husband is a piece of shit. He doesn't deserve you."

"Who is this? Why would you say those things?" The voice's cadence and pitch felt vaguely familiar, but Alice couldn't bring a name to the forefront of her tongue. "Stop calling. You're starting to scare me. I will report you to the police for harassment." The voice didn't need to know John's position on informing the police.

The only response was the click of a hang-up.

She wouldn't mention the phone call to John. She briefly debated calling the police to make a report. Alice sighed. It wasn't worth the argument with John. He was probably right and the culprit was a neighborhood kid who had gotten ahold of their phone number. That fact didn't make the calls any less unsettling. Especially when she happened to be by herself at the house.

As for when John would come home tonight?

He would get home when he got home.

Chapter Five

Natalie

Natalie's hand trembled as she slowly pushed the call button on her cell phone. The words Alice Smith appeared across the front screen along with a timer showing the length of the phone call. She heard Alice pick up the phone on the other side. Natalie remembered Alice's old landline phone that John refused to give up.

"Hello? Hello? Who is this?" Alice said. Natalie heard the words through a tunnel. Alice again asked, "Hello? Hello?"

Natalie's mouth dried up and her lips couldn't form any words.

"This is the seventh time you have called here. I'm getting tired of it. Say something or stop calling," Alice demanded. Natalie listened to Alice prattle on about an old prank call joke. A dad joke the kids called them.

Natalie opened her mouth to say, "Alice, I slept with your husband. I slept with John." Once again, the words wouldn't rise to the occasion. Instead, she said, "Your husband is a piece of shit. He doesn't deserve you."

"I'm hanging up. Please stop calling. It's starting to scare me." Alice hung up the phone. Natalie heard the satisfying click of an ended phone call on the old landline phone. A noise that would slowly go away into the past.

Natalie looked around her shabby apartment. She saw the worn and frayed edges of the carpet. The couch she sat on smelled of someone's dog. She couldn't move. Her limbs leaden and dead. She had caused this. She had lost her entire life over John Smith.

*   *   *

Eighteen months ago

"Well, hello, beautiful. What are you doing here by yourself? It must get lonely standing out here with everyone else inside making merry," John said.

"Making merry? Who says that?" Natalie laughed.

"I was being cute. Didn't you recognize that?"

"Oh, now that it's been pointed out to me, I definitely realize you're being cute," Natalie said.

"I thought so," John smiled and tilted his head.

Natalie and John had been seeing each other for a little over three weeks. Her heart still fluttered when she saw him enter the room. She smiled uncontrollably when she saw him.

The pit of her stomach hurt like an ulcer when she looked at his wife, her best friend, Alice.

John moved and stood so that his little finger barely brushed hers. "What are you doing? Someone might see us," she breathed out.

"Who? Your husband? When's the last time he even looked at you? He hasn't seen you in years," John scoffed.

"What about Alice?"

"Alice is fine. She's inside trying to be a good hostess. She won't notice anything I don't want her to notice."

"That's mean."

John leaned in closer. Natalie could smell his aftershave. "Sometimes the truth is mean," he said.

"We shouldn't be doing this," Natalie whispered.

"We aren't doing anything. We're just standing here. It's what friends do."

"I'm not talking about right now. I mean, I am talking about right now, but that includes everything. We shouldn't be doing any of this," Natalie said.

"You want to. We can stop whenever you want to," John linked his finger through hers. "I don't think you really want to."

"I don't. I do. I can't. This is crazy. I can't stop thinking about Alice."

"You don't think about your husband?"

"He doesn't care about me. I don't think he's cared for a while. Alice cares."

"I don't want to talk about my wife. She's fine. She prefers things this way."

"How can you say that?" Natalie asked.

"Alice always works better in a bubble. I provide the bubble. Why are we talking about this? Why aren't we talking about how sexy you would look in some lingerie?"

Natalie fell into John's words and forgot about Alice. She hadn't been happy in a long time. The kids took so much time. Her husband took so much time. She didn't have any time for herself anymore.

John made her happy. Was it selfish to want to be happy?

Chapter Six

Jessica

John left the conference room where Jessica had organized the trial files and paperwork into piles. She heard him speaking into his phone in the hallway. She pressed her ear to the door, trying to hear what he was saying or to whom he was speaking. Based on the time of day and his soft tone, she assumed it was his wife.

She and John now met regularly after work for dinner or drinks, ostensibly to work on various cases. It began a couple of weeks ago and escalated quickly. She knew what John expected and happily provided it for him.

"Was that your wife?"

"Yes. I always try to talk to Alice on the phone if I'm working late. I don't want her to worry or to take the time to make dinner if I won't be home."

"Alice. That's your wife's name? It's nice that you think of her."

"It isn't *nice*. It's called marriage. If I didn't pick up, Alice would continue to call and call. She'll leave a ton of voicemails and take up all the space on my phone, so that no one else can get through to leave a message. It's just easier to answer the call the first time or to call her early in the night. I don't feel the need to discuss my wife right now." He looked Jessica up and down before he asked, "Have you called for dinner yet? I'm thinking sushi. What's that place I like?"

"Happy Fish. I will make the call now. How would you like to pay for it?"

John answered, "Charge the client."

"The client?"

John laughed. "Of course. We're working on his case, right?"

"Do you want anything special?"

"Nope. Thanks for asking. Whatever you order will be great."

She dialed the number and put in the order. She watched John as he stepped over to the conference table and began to comb through the notes she had arranged. He was tall. Broad-shouldered. A full head of salt and pepper hair that he wore just long enough to not be described as military. He was thick-waisted, but many men gained some weight as they aged. She viewed it as a sign of comfort and a well-led life. He was several years older than all the other men she had dated.

Boys that she had dated.

"Do we have any sake for our meal?" He asked.

"No, we don't."

"You didn't order any?" he seemed cross.

"They don't deliver alcohol, but I can run out and get some," Jessica explained.

John sighed. "Please do. Make sure to charge that to the client as well. We will expense it later. If they want us working these hours, they can pay for it."

John never paid for a meal if the client should be paying for it. She liked that about him. He understood his worth. Most men didn't or were simply worthless. Jessica assumed, like most women, she had always been attracted to power.

On her way out the door, she began to think about her prior relationships. None had lasted longer than six months. Adam had been the longest. Her favorite. She still Facebook "stalked" him which doesn't really count as "stalking" because they were Friends. She had Friended him using a fake account with a profile picture of her niece's cat. He had just posted a photo of his new child's Halloween costume.

Underneath the photo, she commented, "What a cute, sweet pea!"

He replied, "Isn't he, though?" It felt nice that they could still be friends after the break-up.

She had met Adam while working on her paralegal certificate. Her day job as a receptionist at Markham & West, PLLC, brought her into daily contact with Adam and other members of the firm. He occasionally brought her flowers, never failed to compliment her, and dropped off little gifts that he thought she would enjoy. Eventually, he provided weekend trips and late dinners on the weekend.

Adam was married, but she preferred to date married men. Complications arose less often. Another woman had broken these men of most of their bad habits. Jessica didn't have to entertain them constantly. They could come to her home and she would cook dinner for them. She didn't have to worry about a man marking his territory like a dog. She had never been the type of girl to fantasize about the perfect wedding and the perfect relationship. She knew those things didn't exist. All she wanted was a sexual relationship that wasn't too demanding of her time and some company when she so chose.

Well, she used to just want that. Every year she got older…

When Adam's wife became pregnant with their second child, he broke off the relationship with Jessica. She remembered the conversation vividly. She lay naked in the hotel bed. As he rolled over to get out of bed, he said, "Jessica, what we're doing isn't right. It isn't fair to my wife. It isn't fair to my children. This isn't the man that I want to be. I want to be proud of my life and the way I lived it. I'm sorry to do this to you…like this. It's not fair to you, either. I promise this is going to be for the best. Please understand how hard this is for me."

She reacted in the normal way and threw the flowers, including the vase, he just bought her at his head. She screamed, "Fuck you! I hate you. You can't just get rid of me. *I* decide when we're done. *Not* you. Fuck you. You don't get to decide."

Adam pulled on his pants and left the room to the tune of Jessica's screaming, "*I* decide. Fuck you. *I* decide. You are nothing!"

Her relationship with John was completely different from the one she had with Adam. John understood her. She never needed to explain herself. John understood what she wanted just from a look she gave him. He really cared for her. John was the first man that she thought might be 'the one.'

The liquor store was about a ten-minute walk from the office. Glad that she had grabbed her sweater before heading out, Jessica pulled it a little tighter around her slim body. The air had a hint of the winter briskness coming, but the cold season hadn't quite gotten a fingerhold yet. In a few more weeks, she would have to take a car because it would be too cold to walk.

Jessica walked into the store, pleasantly jingling the strip of bells that hung from the corner of the door. The Pakistani proprietor called out, "Good evening, my young friend! We have a lovely Bordeaux that has just come in. I set aside a couple of bottles for you and your sweetheart." She nodded and waved to him, forgetting his name.

"Thank you," Jessica answered. "Today, I need a sake though." She pulled up a picture on her phone that she had taken of the last bottle John had bought and showed it to the man. The man hurried out from behind the counter to show Jessica the sakes. She selected a moderately priced forty-dollar bottle. John preferred the Junmai daiginjo, generally considered the maker's best offering. "I think I will go ahead and get those bottles of wine as well," she said, figuring that would make up for not knowing the proprietor's name. She would leave them at the office and save a trip back as the weather grew wintry.

She bundled the bottles into her re-usable grocery bag and headed back towards the office. As she was coming upstairs, she glanced at John's car. He drove a new black BMW Crossover. She watched a curvy female form throw paint all over the car.

She walked to the elevator. When she got off on the 20th floor, she started yelling, "John! John! Your car! Oh my God! Your car!"

Chapter Seven

Detective Morrison

ost people think they are smarter than the police. They appreciate a policeman's "service" to the community, but secretly think that if the police officer was smarter, he or (let's be fair) she would have chosen a different profession. That said, most people still expect the dumb policeman to solve all of their problems in a time of crisis.

So many reasons exist as to why "your policeman" can't solve a crime. The lowest rung is that the police detective simply isn't intelligent enough. That accounts for maybe ten percent. The biggest percentage? At least seventy percent? People do not cooperate with the police. People won't answer questions truthfully. They evade. Even when they have no reason to evade, they do.

People won't step up as witnesses. The Kitty Genovese effect. Kitty Genovese supposedly had been raped and stabbed outside her New York apartment while thirty-eight bystanders watched and did nothing. Although the story, itself, has been largely debunked. Most people believe the NY Times made the story up or, at a minimum, conducted substandard reporting. The fact remains that the more people available to witness or to stop an incident, the less likely anyone saw anything or would step in to help, which generally equates to the police looking stupid.

Very few crimes are genuinely unsolvable. They exist, but to have an unsolvable crime, a criminal mastermind must be at work.

Morrison didn't believe in criminal masterminds.

"Excuse me! Excuse me! Does anyone actually work here?" Morrison looked over and saw a middle-aged, paunchy blowhard yelling at the desk sergeant. He sighed. Next time he got married, he needed to make sure there was a pre-nup that was expertly crafted in his favor, instead of handing his life's worth over to the next ex-Mrs. Morrison. Working overtime to deal with these assholes was not worth the hassle.

He looked around the sparse lobby. Seeing no other detectives or patrol officers in sight, Morrison walked over, "My name is Detective Morrison. Can I help you?"

"Yeah, you can help me. Where the hell were you guys tonight around eight p.m.?" the Blowhard asked.

"Likely answering calls to service, but how exactly can I help you? I assume something happened around eight tonight?"

The woman next to Blowhard fretfully stroked his arm. "John, calm down. It's just a car. Everything will be ok."

Morrison noted the massive rock on her ring finger, the large pearls encasing her neck and a wild head of curls silhouetting her face.

Blowhard continued, "My car has been destroyed. I called the police and waited FOR OVER AN HOUR for you assholes to come out and take a report. Then what happens? You send a patrol officer that I'm not sure has even graduated from high school. Also, a patrol officer? My car costs more than her yearly salary! I need to speak to a real detective. My name is John Smith and I want someone to do something about my car!"

Morrison went to sit down at his desk and motioned for Blowhard and his wife to follow him. Over his shoulder, he called, "Mary, if you've got the name he keeps screaming so loudly that God can hear him, could you please get me the report on this incident, please? I will go ahead and do the follow-up." As much as he didn't want to deal with this asshole, he didn't want to leave it to a patrol officer. The problem was above their pay grade.

"Let me guess, someone threw pig's blood on your car and now you're mildly irritated," Morrison suggested while motioning for the couple to sit down at his messy desk.

"Is there actually something wrong with you? Pig's blood? I am talking about my vehicle. Are you a detective? Or just impersonating one?"

"Sorry, I was trying to make a joke, but I'm obviously not that funny."

"Obviously."

Morrison took a deep breath. "I'm First Detective Morrison. I'd like to help you. What's your name, sir?"

"John Smith."

"For real, what's your name?"

"Can we dispense with the funny stuff? My name is John Smith."

"Ah, sorry. I apologize. It's been a long day." Morrison rubbed his hand over his face.

"John, give him a chance. Tell him what happened. He's going to try and help us," the lady pleaded.

Blowhard took another steadying breath and began, "Look. Someone bashed in the windows to my car and wrote the word 'Pig' all over it."

"So, I wasn't super far off with the pig's blood joke, huh?" Blowhard stared but made no other overt movements. Morrison continued, "I understand that vandalism can be unnerving..."

"Unnerving? Do you think that I would be here if I were just unnerved? We have been receiving death threats through the mail and by phone. Someone has thrown a rock through my living room window and now this. Yeah, I guess you could say I'm a little unnerved."

Morrison perked up at these revelations. "Have you filed any reports before?"

Blowhard waved his hand through the air. "Yes, yes. When the rock went through the window. We came in, not that it did any good."

"No other reports? Who did you initially file with?"

"No other reports. They seemed inconsequential. I can't be expected to remember a name. Why don't you just look it up in the system? I assume that you have a system to track reports?"

The lady piped up. "Death threats? John, what are you talking about? You never told me anything about death threats." Blowhard continued to stare straight at Morrison. Ignoring her.

Morrison picked up the lady's thoughts. "You found death threats to be inconsequential? Most people get a mild sense of concern when they're on the targeted end of a threat."

"Are you questioning the decisions that I make about my life?" Blood began to rush into Blowhard's face. He placed both hands flat on the desk and he pushed away.

"Nope, not at all. Makes perfect sense to me that it sounds like you're being harassed and chose not to report it. I mean, really, what could the police possibly do?" Morrison's voice dripped sarcasm. "Do you have any idea who could be doing this?" Morrison tried to ask the last question sincerely.

"None at all. None at all. Is there a vending machine somewhere? I need some water," Blowhard said.

Morrison gestured in a vague direction.

"Alice, sweetheart, would you mind?"

The lady obediently left her seat and started moving in the direction indicated.

"Look, I don't want my wife to hear this, because I love her, you know?"

Morrison closed his eyes, already anticipating Blowhard's next statement.

"Once in a while, I step outside my marriage. One of the young ladies..."

"One of?" Morrison interjected.

"Yes, one of. Do you have a problem, or do you want to make another snarky comment? Can I finish what I was saying before my wife gets back?"

Morrison made a move along hand motion.

"One of the young ladies became a little too infatuated with me. Alice doesn't know this."

"I'm sure she doesn't," Morrison responded dryly.

Blowhard's eyes narrowed. "She doesn't," he repeated emphatically. "I believe that young lady has repeatedly been calling my house. She doesn't leave a message, but it's still frightening my wife. She's the one behind all of this."

"What's her name?"

"Look, I really don't want to get her into trouble or go to court or anything like that."

"You mean you don't want to do anything that means your wife could possibly find out about your affairs? What makes you think she doesn't already know? Is she that stupid?"

Blowhard stood up immediately, "Don't you DARE insult my wife."

"I'm the one insulting your wife? Seriously? I'm the one." Morrison nodded his head. "You don't think that you're mildly insulting her by cheating on her?" Morrison felt his voice rising as he continued to talk to Blowhard. "You don't think that you're insulting her by pretending that your farce of a marriage is okay?"

"Who the actual fuck are you to speak to me like this? I want to speak to your commander! You cannot speak to me in this manner. I won't allow it. You don't know shit about my marriage."

"John, is everything ok? I have your water." The lady in question returned. Her eyes darted quickly between Morrison and her husband.

Blowhard was red in the face, sweat marks beginning to show through his expensive shirt. He started to jot something down on a piece of paper that he grabbed from Morrison's desk. "Here you go, asshole. Let's see if you're worth the tax money I pay every year." Blowhard shoved the paper at Morrison. His eyes daring Morrison to object.

Morrison heard the woman murmuring to Blowhard, but couldn't make out the words. "Come on, Alice. We're finished here. If anything comes out of this, I will be shocked. We pay for all of this shit. We pay for it. You know that, right? We pay for it. This whole fucking decrepit police station. They can't even be bothered to treat us, the taxpayers, civilly." Blowhard took hold of his wife's upper arm and was leaving the squad room. Morrison listened to him complain the whole way out.

Morrison internally counted his years until his child support payments ended. Sighing, he then prayed to any god that would listen for his ex-wife to remarry so he could put an end to the alimony. Neither event was likely to occur soon. He was stuck at this job. Dealing with entitled assholes who apparently paid his salary.

He picked up the paper Blowhard threw at him.

Just one name on it.

Natalie McInroe.

Chapter Eight

Alice

Alice returned from retrieving a bottle of water from the vending machine after taking approximately ten minutes to find the appropriate area. The Detective had not been very forthcoming about the machine's location. He could easily have given a description. It's in the northwest corner of the lobby. Or, just look to your left as soon as you take ten steps out of the hallway. A Detective should be more precise and more calculated with his words.

Alice wasn't sure this "Detective" was going to be able to help them anyway. His gray hair looked overdue for a cut. His suit hadn't been purchased any time in the last decade, judging from the worn patches at the elbows. He stank of cigarettes. He kept making ridiculous jokes. She guessed they were jokes, because the Detective kept saying they were.

Honestly, it was no wonder that John lost his temper.

As she returned to the Detective's desk with John's water, she could hear yelling. She quickened her pace. "John, is everything ok? I have your water."

John scribbled something down on a post-it note he had grabbed from the Detective's desk. The whole time he ranted, "We pay your salary. I can't believe this is how I'm being treated. Do you know who I am? Do you know who my wife is? Who her family is? Don't treat me like some jerk who came in off the street."

"John, it's time to go. We can revisit this later," she softly tried to cajole him into leaving. "John, it's so late. I'm so tired. You woke me up from my sleep to take me to the police station. I wanted to come because I am so worried about you. But now, I'm starting to fade. Let's go home. We have so much to do tomorrow." She kept quietly whispering in his ear.

John glanced her way and continued, "I'm going to call the police chief tomorrow about how I've been treated. My wife is fucking exhausted and all you people can seem to do is clown around."

"John, let's go. You aren't helping anything."

"Come on, Alice. We're finished here. If anything comes out of this, I will be shocked. We pay for all of this shit. We pay for it. You know that, right? We pay for it. This whole fucking decrepit police station. They can't even be bothered to treat us, the taxpayers, civilly."

John grabbed Alice's upper arm, squeezing so hard that fingerprint-sized bruises would appear in the morning. He frog marched her out of the police station. Never loosening his grip. Never letting go.

"Well. You don't have to act this way. You're hurting me."

"I don't know who that guy thinks he is. My God. What do you even think he makes in a year? Thirty thousand? He's going to be completely useless. We shouldn't even have bothered," John muttered to himself.

"You do know that I said we should just call the insurance company. We have no proof or any information about who did this. We should have just filed a police report like we did with the rock. YOU insisted on heading to the police department. Also, do you know what you sound like when you completely misjudge how much someone is making? I guarantee he's making at least sixty-five thousand, anyway." Alice tried to pull out of his grip once more. "Let go of my arm! You're hurting me!"

John pulled his hand away as if he had burned it. "Alice...please just...please just let me be for a minute. I'm very upset right at this second. I feel strongly that nobody wanted to listen to me. I'll calm down and call that detective back. Promise." He stopped for a second, "I highly doubt they are going to do anything about my car. It *is* shameful the way these," he raised his fingers in quotation marks, "police officers' take care of this community. I'm going to have a sit-down talk with the chief next week. I can't be the only person having these kinds of problems, but I guess it's going to be up to me to fix the department."

Closing her eyes and scrunching her face, Alice could only imagine what that conversation would entail. Maybe, she would call her father and ask him to speak to her husband. Talk some truth into him. Alice asked, "Will you apologize for how you treated him?"

"Sure will."

Alice had doubts, but kept her opinion to herself.

Battles worth fighting and all that.

*   *   *

That evening at 10:03 pm, Alice called Natalie again. She called three times before she just left a message.

"Hey Natalie, it's Alice. I just wanted to talk to you. It's been a long day. John's car was vandalized and he started screaming at people at the police station. He was just upset. I need to figure out how to do a better job of calming him down. I got one of those calls again the other night. You know the one where someone calls, but no one is on the other line. It's the seventh phone call. The dates and times are erratic. This particular one was twenty percent longer than the previous ones. It's starting to scare me. I don't know what's going on and I don't know what to do. I really need you right now. Call me. Please."

Alice sat on the couch alone after her phone call and stared at the wall. Her eyes gazed at a family picture she had hung up the previous year, but not seeing it. John had gone to bed about twelve minutes previously mumbling about incompetence. She tried to call Ryan already. He picked up the phone, but was at a nightclub and she could barely hear him. She closed her eyes to make a silent prayer. She thought, *Please, God. Please let Natalie still want to be my friend and tell me what I did to upset her so much.*

She stood up and went into the bedroom hoping that answered prayers actually existed.

*   *   *

Alice called Detective Morrison back the next day and left a message: "Detective, this is Alice Smith. I want to apologize for my husband's behavior. He doesn't usually get that worked up. That said, how do I get a copy of the police report? Is that something you can get for me or do I need to file some paperwork? I looked online, but I couldn't find the correct document number. We need the paperwork for the insurance company."

Her next phone call was to the rental car company who promptly answered their phone. "Hi, my name is Alice Smith and I need a rental. Mmm. Hmmm. No...today. As soon as possible. A Kia? Oh, no, that won't work. Do you have a BMW or something of that caliber? Oh really? Dang. A Honda. Well, if it's reliable, you know, and they have an HTSB rating of A+ for head-on impact. Yup, here's my credit card information...I'll be down in an hour to pick it up."

To the insurance company: "I've already requested the police reports and I will get them to you as soon as possible. No, they don't have a suspect yet. We prefer to use the dealership for these sorts of things. Is that a problem? They have a much better warranty system. Oh. I understand. I didn't realize you had a contract with that shop. Don't worry. We don't live in a neighborhood with high vandalism rates. Will you just send them the check? I think that would be best. Thanks so much. You've been so accommodating."

And lastly, "I know it's last minute, but I need a reservation for two people at 7 PM. By the North facing window, please. You don't? This is Alice Smith. I used to be Alice Patrick. My father speaks very highly of your restaurant. But if you can't get us in tonight, I will just let him know that you can't accommodate his daughter. Wonderful! Seven would be perfect. Thank you so much. Looking forward to dinner. Yes, actually. A Bordeaux would be perfect, but make sure it's at least sixty-five percent cabernet. Yes. Yes. Left bank Bordeaux would be best. No, I don't understand. That's what my husband would prefer. Money is no matter."

She called John: "Hi honey. I know yesterday was crazy and you seemed so stressed. I took care of the rental, the insurance company and requested a police report. Also, I made reservations for seven at Les Nomades because I know how stressed you were. No working late! Come see your wife and let's have an amazing dinner! Love you! Check out Prague!"

*   *   *

Alice walked into Les Nomades at 6:57 pm. She had taken an extra five minutes with her hair this evening and slipped into a pale blue dress. She wanted to look nice for her date with John.

"Welcome, madame! It is always a pleasure to see you! Mrs. Smith, I have a beautiful table reserved for you by the window. It is as you requested, yes?" the maître d' greeted.

Alice nodded. "Yes. Thank you. I'm glad you could accommodate us. My husband will be meeting me in a few minutes."

"Would you like to wait for him here or would you prefer to be seated?"

"I'll sit at the table, please."

"Let me show you the way. Would you like me to open the bottle of wine you ordered or would you like a separate glass while you wait?"

"I'd like to start with a glass of wine. Please make it a French white."

"It would be my absolute pleasure." He motioned for Alice to follow him to the requested table. Alice nodded in appreciation. It was precisely where she wanted to sit. More importantly, it was exactly where John would want to sit. She waited for the maître d' to pull out her chair and sat in it. She smiled at him and accepted the menu.

She looked through the menu for three minutes and then glanced at her watch. 7:04 pm. John wasn't exactly late, but he wasn't prompt. A waitress came by and dropped off the requested glass of wine. Alice smiled at her and went back to looking at the menu.

After three more minutes, the waitress came back to the table. "Are you still waiting or would you like to order an appetizer?"

"I'm still waiting, thank you."

Alice looked through the window and found herself daydreaming. Occasionally, she would have a sip of wine. At 7:20, her phone began to vibrate in her purse. She looked at the caller ID and saw it was John.

"Where are you? I've been at the restaurant for twenty-three minutes," Alice stated when she answered the call.

"Alice. I'm so sorry, but I won't be able to come to dinner. I got caught up at work and there's not much I can do about it."

"I asked you to make sure you weren't late. Remember? I specifically asked you."

"Honey, this isn't my fault. I didn't get your message right away. Sometimes I have to work late. I can't help it. What is so difficult about that for you to understand? My time isn't always my own."

"I know. I just really wanted to spend some time with you. I requested your favorite table and a special bottle of wine for you."

John groaned, "Alice, I'm sorry. What else do you want me to say? Bring home the bottle and we will enjoy it tomorrow. I promise we will spend more time together. I'm crossing my heart right now, even though you can't see it."

Alice heard female laughter in the background. "Who is that?"

"Who's who?"

"That person laughing. Who's laughing?"

"Oh, that's just Jessie. She stayed late to help me out. Don't worry about it. You stay at the restaurant and have a nice meal though, ok? Just take a little Alice time and enjoy yourself. Forgive me for being a bad husband, pretty please?"

"Forgiven. Just don't forget about me when you are shuffling all of your work priorities," Alice sighed.

"I never would," John promised as he ended the phone call.

Chapter Nine

Detective Morrison

"Officer Nyla, thanks for getting back to me," Morrison stated. A quick phone call to the responding officer about Smith's vandalism would put Morrison's mind at ease that he followed up the complaint the way he promised. Not to mention cover his six, if the asshole followed up on his promise to call the Chief.

"Not a problem, Detective. What can I do for you?" Morrison could hear tires and honks from traffic noise over the phone. Clearly, Nyla pulled a traffic duty assignment today. Morrison was sure she would be happy to chat and relieve some of the boredom of the mundane assignment.

"I have your report in front of me about an incident last night with a John Smith. No joke. The guy's actual name. I ran him through DMV, because I thought he had to be lying. DL photo is out of date, but it's definitely the same jackass," Morrison explained.

"That guy was a total ass. I completely remember him. He kept trying to tell me how to do my job." She started to mimic Blowhard, "Make sure you take a picture of the front. You need to do a better job. I pay my taxes."

"Oh, I totally get it. The usual, 'I pay your salary bit.' Love the life of a public servant. He did that with me, too. I have just a few follow-up questions. Can you give me just a quick overview of the scene?" Morrison continued.

"I arrived within an hour of his call. All he could do was scream at me the whole time. His car was a total mess, though. Pretty lady at his side. She didn't say much."

"The lady's name was Alice Smith?"

"No, Jessica something. Hang on, let me check my notes."

"Don't bother. That's interesting in and of itself. Did they seem friendly?"

"More than. For sure. I assumed it was a girlfriend, but I didn't ask. He didn't introduce her or provide any more information about her. Eventually, he asked her to leave and a different, mousier woman showed up."

"Huh. Must have dismissed the girlfriend so the wife wouldn't see her. What were your thoughts on the incident with the car?" Morrison asked.

"Words painted all over the car and windows smashed, but no damage that wasn't cosmetic. Looked like a former girlfriend had a temper tantrum. That was the feeling I got, especially with his attitude. He cared, but didn't care. I don't know how to explain it. Like he was acting? I dunno. He seemed angrier that he had to take time out of his life to deal with the problem than that the problem existed in the first place." Officer Nyla paused, then continued, "This dude wanted me to get crime scene unit out and fingerprint his car. I laughed in his face."

"How did he take that?"

"Not very well. Not very well at all. He kept asking when the 'real' police were going to show up. I told him that I'd been an officer for over four years. He told me that was cute, but he wanted to talk to a detective."

"About a misdemeanor property report?"

"Yup. I told him it was doubtful that anything would come of it. He would be better off taking a copy of my report and sending it to his insurance agency."

"That's probably true."

"The next thing he demanded was to pull security footage. I could follow up with that, I guess. Half the time those cameras are just for show."

Morrison groaned, "Don't worry about it. I'll take over from here. I'll go ahead and contact the building to security and request any video, if there is any. I've got a name to follow up on as well."

"A name from him?"

"Yeah."

"Huh. He wouldn't tell me anything." She paused as a horn sounded in the background, "Detective, is there a reason you wanted to talk to me about a simple misdemeanor? The dude is a jerk. I'm pretty sure that whatever happened, he deserved what he got ten-fold. Doesn't seem interesting enough to warrant your involvement."

"It's really not. He just came down to the station hollering holy hell. I'm just following up, so I can tell him that I did. Trying to head off what I'm sure is going to be a complaint. He strikes me as that kind of guy."

"Understood. Let me know if you need anything else, Detective."

Morrison hung up the phone. He leaned back in his chair and steepled his fingers. Nothing particularly interesting came from this conversation. Seemed like Blowhard had a little side piece at the scene. The vandalization of the car was likely a gift from a former mistress.

Morrison wondered how much the wife knew about her husband's habits. In his experience, the wife usually knew something, even if she chose to ignore it.

He couldn't understand why a woman would put up with that type of shit from a man. Morrison's wife hadn't. That's why he wrote those checks every month. Called his kids on the phone once a week instead of seeing them in person. Morrison had found that rich people received more consideration, more latitude. Even from their own family.

Morrison shook his head. A person could never tell what went on inside another's marriage. It was sometimes best not to speculate.

He made a note to call about the security footage after lunch and track down an address for the mysterious Natalie McInroe.

*   *   *

"Usually, we require a subpoena before we hand out security footage. It's just to protect us, but I wouldn't bother with taking the time to request it. I just watched the video and all you can see is someone dressed in a black hoodie throwing paint onto the car," the building's security officer stated to Morrison.

"Does the person look male or female? Can you tell?"

"Not a hundred percent, but the body shape looks female to me. Small. Curvy."

"I really would like to see that video. I will get a subpoena out to you ASAP. How soon would you be able to release it to me?"

"I will go ahead and record it onto a thumb drive for you, so it will be ready when you get the paperwork in order."

"I appreciate it."

Morrison sat back in his chair. The only new information gained was that an unknown person had been recorded vandalizing Smith's vehicle. He wanted to see the footage to determine if he could tell if the perpetrator was female or not. It might be enough for him to convince Natalie McInroe to confess.

Chapter Ten

Jessica

"I never bring people to my home, but I thought you could use a homemade dinner for once. I remember you saying that your wife doesn't cook much." Jessica felt comfortable in her small, brightly lit kitchen. She opened the spice cabinet and pulled the ones she needed for dinner. She wore a sundress instead of her standard corporate blouse and skirt, making her feel lighter and sexier.

"She cooks. I'm just not home much, so she doesn't bother to do it just for herself. She just claims it's lonely to cook when I'm not home," John replied.

John came up behind her and pulled her hair from its ubiquitous bun. He kissed the nape of her neck. "You know I like it best when you have your hair down. Are you sure you don't want to put dinner off until later?"

She giggled. A most un-Jessica-like giggle. "No. If we don't eat now, everything will be ruined. I hate being wasteful."

He turned her around, running his hands over her body, "I'll show you wasteful."

"John!"

They ate later than expected that night.

*   *   *

After showering together, Jessica asked, "Why don't you just stay the night?"

"Jessie, we've been over this. You know I can't do that. Alice would get suspicious."

Jessica twirled her hair between her fingers. "Don't you want to spend time with me?"

"Of course, I do! But, I have a wife and it's important to keep her happy."

"Why?"

John looked confused. "I don't understand. What do you mean by why? For one, she's my wife. Two, her family would kill me for not keeping up appearances. Three, you know what her maiden name was?"

"What?"

"Patrick. Of the Lakeside Patricks."

Jessica shrugged.

"Don't you know what that name means in this town? Daniel Patrick? That's Alice's father. If he whispers 'boo!,' I don't have a job, a house, or any kind of life. I wouldn't have anything! Without their money, Alice and I wouldn't be as comfortable as we are right now. I'm not a partner in the firm yet as my father-in-law happily likes to remind me."

"You don't own the house you live in?"

"Of course, we own it. Alice's parents just gave us some money for the down payment and helped to negotiate a surprisingly good deal for us. We still have a mortgage like normal people," he paused and rolled his eyes. "I don't know why you are so interested in my wife."

"I'm not interested in your wife. Your married life doesn't have anything to do with me. I just asked you some questions. I feel like our relationship would be easier without her. Don't you think so?"

John narrowed his eyes. "Jessie, we don't have a relationship. We have an arrangement. There's a difference. Remember we talked about this from the beginning? We spend some time together. I buy you nice things. We enjoy each other's company. No strings. No emotions."

She flapped her right hand in the air. "I know, I know. I'll see you tomorrow."

"This isn't a joke. It's not a relationship. Do you need me to pay you? I don't mind. I know you don't make that much money." John opened his wallet, "I have plenty and I enjoy spending it on you."

"Don't you mean that your wife has plenty of money?" Jessica asked slyly, making John wince. "I'm not a whore. I don't need *money* from you. I do like sapphires, though."

John grabbed her around the waist. "No money, but you like sapphires. I'll see what I can do. Can we talk work for one second?"

Jessica nodded her assent.

John continued, "Make sure you have that file on the Nelson case ready, please. I have to present it to the fucking partners in the morning."

"No problem. I will get in early and make sure that you have everything that you need."

John left through the front door. She could hear him in the hallway. "Hi, Honey. I'm on my way home now. I know. I know. I absolutely will tell them I need more time for my family. You are right. No. No. I had dinner. See you soon. Ummmm...Cancun?"

Jessica stood still and listened to him until he got in the elevator. She busied herself with cleaning the kitchen. Leftovers in the fridge for lunch tomorrow. Wiping down the counters. Setting the coffee timer for the morning. Trying not to think about how easily she was dismissed.

When she finished, she sat on her couch and stared at the TV. She didn't turn it on. She didn't want that kind of distraction. Was it happening again? Was she mistaking convenience for love? For a relationship?

Grabbing her keys off the table, Jessica knew where she wanted to go. There was a house in the suburbs that she visited when she felt particularly unbalanced. It would only take about an hour to get there. Not long at all.

*   *   *

The streets were quiet in the tree-lined suburbs. She sat outside and watched for the occupants that lived in the blue house with white shutters. She could hear a dog barking inside. When had he gotten a dog? It hadn't been here two weeks ago. After an hour, Adam, her last boyfriend, came outside with a medium-sized hound in tow. He must have gotten it from a shelter. It looked too big just to be a puppy.

"I'm just going to take Lucky for a quick walk. I told you getting a dog would be a great way to force me to exercise," he called over his shoulder. Probably to his wife. Jessica had seen the wife several times when she visited the house previously. The wife looked like a wannabe slut. The second pregnancy had exacted a weight toll. Her tight-fitting clothes screamed a refusal to shop for anything new. Everything was too tight and bulged disgustingly in the wrong places.

It was good that Adam started walking every day. He had followed his wife's cues and gained some pregnancy weight. While he was able to manage his diabetes with insulin, exercise and diet played a big part. Clearly, he had stopped going to the gym. The result looked as if he was hiding a basketball under his shirt. Jessica did not find it endearing.

Jessica got out and followed her target. Quickly and quietly. Adam turned left at the first intersection and picked up a neighborhood walking path about halfway down the block. The dog trotted merrily along by his side.

After about ten minutes, the path opened up to a small clearing with a bench. He sat down on it and scratched the dog between his ears. "How long are you planning on following me?"

Jessica started. "I didn't think you could see me or knew I was here."

"I've asked you to stop showing up at my house. Stop parking and watching me. You are scaring my family. I have a restraining order against you. You do understand that I could call the police and have you arrested right now?" Adam sounded tired, not angry.

"You just got the restraining order to make your wife happy. I know that you still want to see me. That you still feel something for me."

"No, Jessica, I don't. I really don't. I want to move on with my family. My wife and I are in counseling. She wanted to leave me. Did you know that?"

"That's great! It's what we wanted!" Jessica smiled.

"What is wrong with you? I mean, honestly. What is wrong with you? Can you hear yourself? I made a mistake. When we had that…that fling. I made a mistake. I thought…I don't know what I thought. I need you to listen to me. I need you to listen."

Jessica and the dog both cocked their heads to the side indicating they were listening. Jessica thought that the dog was just pretending to listen.

"Do. Not. Come. Around. My. House. Again. I will call the police. I will not allow you to break up my family or hurt them in any way," Adam's voice was quiet, but forceful.

"What do you want me to do? Just stop? Just like that?" Jessica snapped her fingers.

"Yes. It's what I wanted you to do over a year ago, when I came to my senses and told my wife about you. You have to stop. I'm serious. I will have you arrested."

"I don't believe you. We only broke up because of the baby. You wanted to try and be a better father, remember? You still want to be with me."

"It doesn't matter what you believe. The truth will be here."

"This whole conversation doesn't matter. I've found someone else. He loves me so much. More than you ever did. I can just tell. A woman's intuition."

"Is he married?"

"Yes."

"Then he doesn't love you. He won't leave his wife."

"You don't know that. You don't know anything about him. He's a completely different person than you! You narcissistic asshole."

"Oh, Jessica," Adam sounded sad. "You're never going to learn. Please go away. Just go back down the trail the way we walked in. I will follow you out. I really don't feel comfortable with you behind me."

Jessica started backing off. "You'll see. You'll see," she whispered.

She could hear Adam following a little way behind her. She didn't look back at him. She went to her car, opened the door and got in. She waited for him to reach his house. Saw him put the dog inside and call out something. Probably, "I'm home" or something mundane to that effect.

He came outside onto the porch. His hands were in his pockets. Shoulders slumped. He stared at her car until she pulled away.

Chapter Eleven

Alice

"How many people are going to be at this thing?" Alice asked. John drove their rented BMW with practiced ease through the busy streets of the city. Alice had followed up with the rental company after John complained about the Honda and secured an appropriate car. Like a true city veteran, he honked several times and threw a few people the finger.

"Ummm…a lot. I really don't know. Over a hundred, I guess. Maybe more? I'm not sure how many people work at the firm. I know that we have twenty-three attorneys. So, you figure that plus spouses and kids. I couldn't tell you how many receptionists, paralegals, and such that we have," John sounded disinterested. "I only show my face because it's expected. You know this isn't my favorite way to spend a Saturday."

"Is Jessie going to be there?"

"I assume so. Why are you interested?"

"Oh, I don't know? Because she's your new paralegal and you have been spending an awful lot of time together," Alice answered.

"What are you implying?"

Alice threw her hands into a calm-down gesture. "I'm not implying anything. For the past few weeks, I think she has seen more of you than I have. I want to meet this mystery woman that is monopolizing my husband's time."

"It's not Jessie. It's work taking up all my time. I'm stressed right now. I have a lot going on. The partners put a lot of faith in me to win this new case. I really don't need you nagging me about my hours and telling me that I don't spend time with you every time I turn around."

"Hold on. Seriously, hold on. I am definitely *not* nagging. You would know if I was nagging. That, I promise. I'm just saying that in the last four weeks, she has been with you sixty-two percent of the time. It will be nice to finally meet your work wife. I'm just looking forward to it. That's all. Please don't jump down my throat."

John put his arm around her shoulders and pulled her in for a quick side hug. "I'm sorry. I just hate that I have to work all of these hours. I'm not trying to take it out on you. Tell you what. Let's just put in our required appearance at this thing and then go on an afternoon date. Anywhere you like. Your pick. I need to spend some time with my wife."

Alice hugged him back. "That sounds great."

John leaned forward and turned up the music and rolled the car window down all the way. "We might as well start getting fresh air before we get to the picnic. Sing along with me, beautiful!" Alice looked over at John as he began to belt "The Piano Man" off-key. Laughing, she started singing along with him as they drove towards their destination.

When they arrived, Alice looked around. "Wow! Your company went all out! I was expecting burgers and dogs, not a completely catered barbecue. Are you sure you still want to leave early?" Alice turned around in a quick circle allowing her skirt to fluff out and follow her. She laughed and pointed towards the petting zoo, the bounce house, and mentally planned for the carnival games. She knew the odds for each game and how to technically win, but her awkward body would never quite cooperate.

John laughed. "Are you kidding? I see enough of these people every day. I don't need to give up time with my wife. I'm glad you're having fun, though." John swiveled his head and finally jerked his head towards a slender woman standing by herself. "There's Jessie if you want to meet her."

Grabbing Alice's hand, he walked towards Jessie. Once his long legs cleared three-quarters of the space between them, he called out, "Jessie! Jessie! This is my wife, Alice. Alice, Jessie."

Alice held out her free hand towards the woman and said, "It's a pleasure to finally meet you. John has said a lot of really nice things about you. We should have you over to the house for dinner one of these nights. It's the least we can do. I'm sure keeping John in check at work takes a lot of energy," Alice rambled good-naturedly.

"Hi, Mrs. Smith. I'm glad to meet you."

"Oh, please. Call me Alice." Alice noted a blush creeping up the younger woman's face. Jessie's honey-colored hair was pulled back into a tight bun. She wore a blazer and three-inch heels. "How can you walk in the grass in those shoes?" Alice wondered aloud.

Jessie twisted her fingers through the pearls gracefully draping her decolletage, "Oh, I just don't feel dressed if I don't have heels on."

"I don't think I have ever been as put together as you are. You look gorgeous. Thirty-seven percent of my time in the morning is spent trying to tame this," Alice patted her hair. "I don't know how John puts up with me."

John lifted Alice's hand to his lips and gently kissed her knuckles. "There is no one in the world that I would rather put up with."

"That's very chivalrous," Alice laughed. "Oh, Jessie, I'm sure you have a ton of other people you would rather chat with besides us. Do you have a boyfriend? Is he here?" Alice looked around.

Jessie's eyes narrowed almost imperceptibly. "I do have a boyfriend and, in fact, he is here."

"We'd love to meet him."

"I'm sure you've already met," Jessie stated.

"Oh? I really don't know that many people from John's office. John's been with the firm for ten years and three months, but I've only been to seven holiday parties and five picnics. We really don't socialize very often with people from his work because he's so busy," Alice mused.

"Well, enough of this," John interrupted. "Jessie, it was good to see you, but I promised my lovely wife a date this afternoon. We are going to blow this pop stand." John started tugging Alice's hand and moving to leave.

Alice allowed herself to be led and called over her shoulder, "Well, bye. It was nice to meet you, Jessie."

When they were buckled in the car, Alice looked over at John. "Was that weird? It felt weird. Did I say something that was insulting? I guess I shouldn't have asked about her having a boyfriend. Maybe that was intrusive? It's so hard for me to meet new people. Is that why you pulled me away so quickly? I wanted her to like me, since you two spend so much time together. I wanted her to feel like part of the family. I'm sorry if I was inappropriate."

"I don't know, babe. Jessie sometimes likes to keep her private life private. To tell the truth, I don't even know who her boyfriend is. I try to make sure a line exists, so she understands the difference between us being co-workers and friends. I think maybe she felt that you were blurring that line."

"Yeah, you're probably right. I was just trying to be friendly. She looked SO uncomfortable. I'm sorry. I just tried too hard. The poor girl was just standing by herself. She looked lonely."

"Meh. Not my problem."

"John! Don't be so mean!" Alice yelled as she smacked him playfully on the shoulder.

"Ok, enough talk about Jessie. Where are we going to spend this perfect Saturday afternoon?"

"How about that super cute new tea house that opened up in town?"

"A tea house?" John screwed up his face.

"You promised."

"You're right. I did promise. Let's go have some super cute tea and talk about... the Maldives."

"The Maldives now. I was thinking of a vacation to Paris," Alice countered.

"Did you remember to renew your passport? I know it was about to expire a while ago. You never know, we might need it on short notice if the winds take us on vacation."

"My passport came in the mail last week. I went ahead and put it in the safe. It would be nice if I could use this one for something instead of letting it expire with no stamps," Alice said pointedly.

"Alice, you know I'm so sorry about the honeymoon. I told you to go on your own. That I wouldn't be mad at you."

They had planned on going to Singapore on their honeymoon. Something dutifully exotic and yet still safe and clean. Two days before their scheduled departure, John received the phone call that would dictate the next ten years of his life. Alice's father had pulled some strings in the legal community. Stanley, Robinson, and Morris PLC offered John a position as a Junior Associate at his current firm. Effective immediately. John started the next day and the honeymoon was canceled. No out-of-country vacations since that point.

"Hmmm... Let's go weigh the pros and cons over a cup of English Breakfast and a scone," John said unenthusiastically.

Chapter Twelve

Natalie

"It's so good to see you! Where have you been? Why are you avoiding Alice and me? What is going on? Give me all of the deets. I just need to know," Ryan demanded.

Natalie ran up to Ryan and felt herself encased in a bear hug. "I can't believe you beat me to the restaurant. You're never early!" She looked around the crowded bar area and felt thankful she had foreseen to make a reservation. Ryan had suggested this place because it was the new "it" scene. She would have preferred something more low-key but didn't want to argue with him.

"I had to be here. Nothing could have stopped me. I need all of the gossip." He held her at arm's length. "You look tired."

Natalie laughed, "How can you insult me like that and I still want to have a drink with you? Ryan, how about we sit down before we get to the nasty business I have to tell you about?"

His eyes gleamed. "Yes. Yes. Yes. First, we will sit down and order. THEN, we will talk about this delicious scandal you have embroiled yourself in."

She sighed, "It's horrible, and I want you to breathe. Once you know everything, you're going to wish you didn't. I promise."

"I can't help it. You know how I feel about gossip. It's my life's blood."

"I think you will feel differently about this."

The waitress came by their table. "Can I have a Cosmopolitan and a lemon drop shot?" Natalie ordered.

"I'll have the same. With waters for both of us," Ryan said. "This must be pretty big news if you had to order that much courage." He wiggled in his seat in anticipation like a three-year-old about to receive a lollipop.

"I don't know how to say this. Can we wait and make small talk until the drinks come? I want a few more minutes before you start to treat me differently."

"I'll never do that. You have my solemn word," Ryan crossed his heart with the index finger on his right hand.

"I wish I could believe you. Tell me something that doesn't matter."

Ryan started to regale her with all of the recent gossip consuming the office. "OMG, you won't believe Lynn..."

Natalie sat back and listened to Ryan's voice wash over her. It felt good pretending nothing had changed.

The waitress set the drinks down on the table. Natalie picked up the shot. "Cheers," she said grimly and threw it back. Ryan echoed her movements.

She took a deep breath and let it out. She opened her mouth to start speaking and promptly closed it again.

"I need you to tell me what's wrong," Ryan said.

Natalie tried again. And again, found herself without words.

Ryan flagged the waitress down. "Sweetie, I want to say that you are rocking those shoes." The waitress smiled. Ryan continued, "Can we have two more shots, please? Real ones this time. Tequila with lime and salt. We need them post haste, please."

The waitress nodded and went to retrieve another round of shots.

"Here's what's going to happen. When the shots get back, you are going to take a deep breath. When you exhale, you are going to tell me the basics of whatever it is that you are so terrified of telling me. Then, we are immediately going to take the next shot. Both of us. No reactions until the shot warms our bellies. Does that sound fair?" Ryan asked.

Natalie nodded in agreement.

The waitress returned and placed the shots on the table.

"I'm going to count you off. On three we take the shots. Ready? One. Two. Three."

Natalie inhaled. When her belly was so full of air that it hurt, she closed her eyes, and let the words tumble out of her mouth, "I slept with Alice's husband, John, for about six months. He broke it off. My husband knows and I'm getting a divorce." She reached blindly for the tequila and drank it, grateful for the burn as it slid down her throat and into her stomach.

Ryan slammed his shot with her. When he was done, he sputtered, "Girl…what?!? I hope you are fucking kidding me."

"I'm not," Natalie said in a tiny voice.

"What? Why? How? Talk to me."

"Do you hate me?" Natalie asked.

"I don't hate you. I don't understand the situation. I'm very upset with you, but I don't hate you. I can't even think. Does Alice know?"

"I don't think so. I haven't told her. I doubt John has told her. Please don't say anything. Please, if you're my friend. Don't say anything."

"I'm her friend, too," Ryan said pointedly.

"You've been my friend longer," Natalie responded.

Ryan stared at her.

Natalie threw up her hands in a defensive motion. "I'm sorry. I shouldn't have said that. I'm the one who's wrong. I should tell her myself. I just don't know how."

"Why don't you tell me exactly what happened and get it all out? Start from the beginning," Ryan requested.

"I don't know where the beginning is. I guess it starts with my husband and me. We were having problems. Yelling at each other. Grating on each other's nerves. Taking each other for granted. We've been married a long time. The kids are involved in everything. It's a twenty-four-hour, round-the-clock job to just get the kids to all their activities on time. Piano lessons. Soccer. Gymnastics," Natalie stopped and considered. "It *was* a round-the-clock job. I'm not in charge of that part of their lives anymore."

"I'm not hearing the part where you had an affair with Alice's husband."

"Just let me tell this the way I need to. Please."

"Fine."

"I felt ignored. Every time we went over to Alice's house, I'd watch how she and John would interact. He always seems so attentive towards her. Hugging her. Kissing her. Whatever she needed, he jumped up to provide it for her."

"I'm not sure that you and I have observed the same things. John's an ass. He treats Alice like a child," Ryan said. Shrugging, he continued, "To be fair, she allows it. Her marriage is her business."

"Well…that's not what I saw or, at least, it's not how I interpreted it. I saw him paying more attention to her than my husband had paid attention to me in a very long time. Eventually, John and I started talking more and more. I can't even pinpoint when I started to have feelings."

Ryan grumbled incoherently. He sipped his drink and nodded for her to continue.

As if in a daze, Natalie continued, "In the middle of a party one night, we both happened to be out on the balcony looking for air. It was so hot inside. He stood next to me and looked me up and down. Like I was a woman. Like I was a desirable woman. He took his pinky finger and put it through mine and took his other hand and…."

Ryan held up his hand in a stop gesture. "I changed my mind. TMI. I do NOT want to know the details. I understand the gist of it. You were lonely. He paid attention to you. You screwed him. But, Alice's husband? Of all people? There was no one else in the whole wide world?"

"I don't hang out with a lot of other people. My social circle isn't that big."

"Neither is Alice's. I know that she's lonely without you and she doesn't understand what she did wrong. You should tell her. She needs to know what kind of person her husband is."

"I can't tell her. I absolutely can't. I don't want her to know what kind of person I really am. I need her to think that I'm good. Please. You can't tell her, either. Promise me. Ryan, promise me that you won't tell her."

"I won't make that promise. I promise to think about it, though. I don't know what to say to you right now. You need to make this better."

"I don't know what to do," Natalie buried her face in her hands.

Ryan sipped his drink and let her cry, but he reached out his right hand over the table. He tapped the table softly with the back of his hand until she took his fingers in hers. Accepting his sympathy.

"I went to see John last week. I told him I was worried about being thrown out of the house when my husband found out about the affair. I asked John for money," Natalie said.

"What did he say?"

"He said everything was my fault and he didn't understand what I expected him to do for me," her breathing hitched. "He said my husband already knew and had filed for divorce."

"He said that mostly because he's a total asshole. You can't expect a jackass to act like a regular person, especially when they don't think they have anything at stake. He knows you won't say anything," Ryan commented.

"I found an apartment over on the west side. It's not a home, but it's somewhere to live. I scraped together a security deposit and the first month's rent, but I have nothing left. Literally. Nothing."

"Are you asking me for money?"

"If I said yes, would you hate me any more than you do now?"

"Again, I don't hate you. I don't want you to suffer, but I won't give you any money until you come clean to Alice. I don't want to hold the burden of your secrets and lies."

"I don't think I can do that."

"Natalie, sweetheart, I will still be your friend. But, I won't lend you money until you do the right thing. Do the right thing. John is never going to help you. He won't. Don't ask him for anything again. I guarantee it will only get worse."

"I don't see how."

"That's what everyone says until it gets worse." He drummed his fingers on the table. "You've put me in a shitty position. I want to be your friend still, but I'm definitely still Alice's friend. I can be like your priest in a confessional. Damn girl, Alice hasn't done anything wrong." He shook his head. "I need to go home and figure out how I can be a friend to both of you."

"I understand," Natalie responded. "Can you...do you..." she stopped.

"What?"

Natalie's cheeks flamed. "Can you pick up the check? I don't have any money."

"Wow. Just wow. I should have guessed. Did you invite me here to confess or to get a free meal?" Ryan asked.

She looked down at her ragged fingernails before she continued, "Both, I guess, if you want me to be honest."

"You waited to tell me what is going on until you needed food."

"Yes."

"I see."

Neither of them spoke for about five minutes. Natalie stared at the remnants of her drink. Ryan ordered another and pounded it.

"Adulteress, I'm gonna lecture you now. I have to for both of us."

Natalie nodded, tears streaming down her face.

"I will pay. Then we are going to the grocery store. I'm buying you groceries. I won't hear any of your nonsense. I won't let you starve. I'm disappointed in you. I feel like a traitor to Alice. I enjoyed this gossip story so much more before I knew it was about Alice and John. Girl, you may have ruined gossip for me. I need you to promise me something, though. First, we're still friends, right?"

"Yes."

"I need you to tell me when you need help. Don't go to John. You and I will figure something out. I won't let you starve. Talk to me before you start turning tricks for a hamburger. I won't let you be homeless. Do you get that?"

"I'm sorry, Ryan. I'm sorry for all of this."

"That isn't a yes."

"I understand what you're saying."

"I hope you do. I really hope you do. I can't believe you would do this. And then make me a party to your... infidelity." Ryan threw a few twenty-dollar bills on the table. "Let's get out of here. I'm going to buy you a week's worth of groceries. There's a grocery store around the block. I don't want to go somewhere where I have to drive. Your confession made me drunk," Ryan said. "For the record, next time you need help or you're in trouble, please let me know before you destroy your life."

Natalie gave him a watery smile. She whispered, "Thank you. Thank you for helping me. For sticking by me. I really need you right now. I wasn't sure if you would help me."

"I will always help you. I will keep your secret. Don't let this secret eat you alive and kill you. Tell Alice. Put it out in the open."

"She won't still be my friend."

"Maybe not. But if *you* are still her friend, you need to tell her."

Natalie sighed and wondered if the old parable was true that two people can keep a secret, only if one of them was dead.

Chapter Thirteen

Alice

lice's father, Daniel Patrick, inherited a small real estate holding. During the last forty years, he turned it into a large real estate empire. After he earned his first million, he married Evelyn Robbs from the Robbs' oil family. Old family money.

Directly after the marriage, he moved his new bride into a 15,000 square foot, six-bedroom, five-bathroom mansion. She immediately hired an interior decorator and began the never-ending task of impressing their friends with their furnishings.

A respectable year into the marriage, Alice Patrick, his first and only child, came into this world. Evelyn Patrick took great pains to not birth any more children. Children, she discovered, stretched out parts of a person's body that would never entirely return to what they used to be. She still peed a little if she laughed too hard. Evelyn Patrick nee Robbs made sure to laugh as little as possible to remedy that situation.

A series of au pairs punctuated Alice's life. Long, leggy blondes drove Alice to and from Catholic school, to and from Mathletes, to and from etiquette school, to and from piano lessons, to and from pottery class, to and from whatever place her mother decided was a necessity for a soon-to-be debutante. Alice would sit quietly and wait for her mother to display her. Once her mother's friends finished cooing over Alice, Evelyn would dismiss Alice and promptly forget about her daughter. She would pour another martini with her society friends, while Alice tried to quietly leave and hide in a nearby closet. Alice had developed a talent for listening to her mother's conversations with her esteemed guests. As her listening talent developed, she became more and more knowledgeable about her own faults.

Alice remembered when she was eight, she and her au pair splashed in mud puddles during a particularly heavy summer rain. She came inside the house dripping wet, hair tangled and mud all over her clothes. Evelyn called out, "Darling, come say hello to my friends."

The au pair answered, "Ms. Patrick, I don't think now is a good time. Let me take her to get cleaned up."

"Don't tell me what to do. If I want my child to come to me, then she will come to me. Alice, come into the parlor." Alice complied, leaving wet, muddy footprints on the beige carpet. When Alice crossed the threshold, Evelyn looked up, "Oh my word! Look at you! What have you done? Go away! GO AWAY!" she screamed. She looked at the au pair, "Don't ever allow this child to look like this again. In front of company! My God. Get her out of here."

Evelyn fired that au pair later that week with the actual cause listed as embarrassment. These young ladies never lasted more than six or eight months. Evelyn always found a reason to fire them, so Alice tried not to get too attached.

Daniel left the running of the house to Evelyn and never weighed in on matters such as the household help. Although, he always seemed to eventually enjoy a glass of scotch in the kitchen with the au pair. That would always signal the beginning of the end of that particular girl's employment.

The only activity Alice, herself, chose and enjoyed was the Mathletes. At twelve, she started on the junior team and moved up quickly to some of the more senior teams despite her young age. She understood math. The numbers always stayed the same. She knew what to expect when she added, subtracted, multiplied, or divided. If she didn't get the correct answer, there was a logical reason for the numbers to be wrong. She could figure out the reason and fix it. The numbers never ignored her or yelled at her or demanded a perfection she could never realize.

As she grew older, she began to see and understand more numbers surrounding her in the world. When she became stressed or agitated, she could count to a thousand and she found it calming. If necessary, she could always start back at one. She used numbers and percentages to help calm her anxiety which helped her to cope with the world around her. She could count until the world made sense.

Evelyn never understood Alice's love of numbers. Alice consistently overheard Evelyn's disappointment in her daughter. Evelyn would tell her friends, "Alice is a pretty enough girl. She could do better if she *cared* and paid attention to something more than a math book. Thank God she is good at something, though, even if it is just math. Daniel and I were starting to worry. I'm not sure that she's ever going to find a decent man to marry her. It's completely possible that she will end up being an old maid. I mean, have you seen that horrible Irish curly hair? Could she look more like a poor person?"

Alice never became angry at her mother for making these sorts of comments. Truth was truth. Alice wasn't ever going to be a society princess. The numbers didn't care. They behaved the same way no matter how much makeup Alice wore, if her socks matched, or how many people liked her.

When she was eighteen, Alice went to the debutante ball to please Evelyn and Daniel. They expected it of her. She danced well enough at the ball to make it through the night, but clumsily enough that no man paid her much mind. She was fine with that. She wanted to go to college. She wanted to find a career path where everything was constant and didn't change. A job she could understand.

She brought John home to meet her parents three months after they had met in the coffee shop. When John and Daniel disappeared into her father's study for a scotch, Alice knew that her parents approved of him. Men allowed to cross the threshold into the infamous study were those deemed worthy enough to hold power and esteem. Alice felt thankful she had brought home one of those men.

"Do we know his family?" Evelyn asked.

"Umm.. he's not from any family you know of," Alice answered.

"Oh. What estate did he grow up at?"

"He's just a regular person, mother. No estate. A lot of people grow up without being a part of the society page."

"He's attractive enough and has good manners. It would be better if we could form a merger with his family. You know, like your father and I did. I suppose everyone has to start somewhere. He has definite potential, though. Let's face it. You aren't going to do much better. I think we can work with him," Evelyn mused. "No, I believe we can work with him. We'll just keep his peasant status on the hush, hush."

"Mother, please."

Evelyn chugged another dirty martini, "I'm just looking out for our best interests, darling. You know that you will inherit a great deal of money someday. I want to make sure you marry someone who will be able to take care of it. Take care of your father's and my legacy."

Alice watched as her mother continued to list John's good traits and bad traits on her fingers. As the good list began to become lengthier, Alice realized that John might be her future. He understood the dynamics of this family in a way that Alice could never grasp. She was born into this family and she still couldn't fit in.

John could help her navigate any choppy familial waters. He could take care of her mentally and physically. He could be the go-between with herself and her parents. Between herself and a society she didn't understand.

He proposed at the Christmas Ball in front of her family. She wore a scratchy dress and a tiara from her Great Aunt Josephine. Both worn at her mother's insistence. "You must look absolutely perfect tonight, darling. Absolutely perfect," her mother said.

"Why?"

"It's the Christmas Ball!" her mother laughed behind her hand, as if she knew something that Alice didn't. "There will be pictures. Both your father and I will be there and I want you to make us proud. Wearing a dress and trying to look pretty is such a small thing for you to do to make your parents happy."

Alice gave in to her mother's demands. She felt herself being plucked and prodded. "You'll thank me," Evelyn kept saying as she nearly gouged Alice in the eye with a mascara wand. "Hand me my martini, dear."

On the night in question, John showed up to the door dressed in a perfectly fitting Gucci tux. "Where did you get the money for that?" Alice asked.

John gave her a peck on the nose. "That's not for you to worry about."

Her father came down and firmly shook John's hand. "A tux looks good on you, boy. I told you it would."

Her mother held out her arms and embraced John in a fake hug, carefully placing both arms on either side of his body, but not touching him. She air-kissed both his cheeks. "You look absolutely charming. Please take this girl and we will meet you at the Ball. You do remember what table to sit at?"

"How could I forget?" John winked. He then whisked Alice out the door.

"What was all that about?"

"Just your parents being your parents. You know how they are."

"Yes, I do. Are they not coming with us?"

"They are. I just wanted to take you separately. I hope you don't mind arriving in a limo." Alice finally looked at the street and saw the driver holding open the door for her.

"John, what's going on?" Alice asked fretfully.

"I wanted this to be a surprise."

"Please. Don't surprise me. Please tell me."

"I asked your father for his permission to marry you on Monday. He granted it," John said.

"To marry me? You want to marry me?"

"Of course! Who wouldn't? Your father agreed and promptly told your mother. She wants everyone to see. She changed their table to number four."

"The one on the upper left. Everyone will see us."

"I believe that's the point."

"I'm going to make a fool of myself," Alice wailed.

"No, you won't. We're going to practice everything. We're going to the park first. At the ball, everything will be the same except others will be watching."

They practiced the routine nine times until Alice felt comfortable. She didn't think she loved him, but sometimes in marriage, love isn't as important as people make it out to be.

When John proposed as rehearsed at the Ball, Alice accepted gratefully. Thanking every god that came to mind that John would be by her side and shelter her from her parents. And shelter her from the world at large.

Alice's early developed habit of eavesdropping on conversations continued to plague her throughout her engagement. She remembered standing in the hallway outside of her father's study in her oversize socks and stretched-out T-shirt. She was supposed to be at the university library studying, but she took the day off to prepare herself mentally for the wedding. She could hear the muffled voices of her father and John.

"What do you mean you don't think you can go through with the wedding?" she heard her father say.

"I just don't feel comfortable. I didn't even know about her 'retreat' until last week. I realized that I might not be able to handle someone with her mental issues. I'm just worried it's going to be too much," John said.

"What do you need?"

"What?"

"What do you need to take care of my daughter? Do you want a down payment on a house? A car? What do you want?"

"I'm not sure what to say."

"Stop beating around the bush. What do you want? If you take care of Alice, I will take care of you. Make sure she's happy. I will make sure that everything else is taken care of."

She heard John swallow, "I can do that."

"If there's ever anything in your marriage that you need, any problems that you need to be taken care of, you come to me first. If you take care of my daughter, I will make sure that you have everything you need."

A tear trickled down Alice's cheek as she turned and left the men to discuss the business of taking care of her. She realized she would always be someone's burden.

Chapter Fourteen

Jessica

"How could you do that to me? I was so embarrassed. Were you trying to make me look like an idiot?" Jessica asked, strangely calm. "I need to understand your motivations, because, right now, I think you're playing some kind of game." She continued to stir the soup for their dinner. She had flirted with John all day to persuade him to come to her house after work. Implying certain things would occur. She wanted to discuss the interaction she and Alice had at the company picnic.

"My wife wanted to meet you, so I introduced you to each other. Should I have just walked on by and completely ignored you? I'm sure my wife wouldn't have asked any questions about that," John said sarcastically. "You were the one who started going on and on about your boyfriend. Who the hell is your boyfriend anyway?"

"Who do you think is my boyfriend?"

"Well, it certainly isn't me. We are not in a relationship. I'm not sure how many times I have to tell you that. We just have some fun now and again. Blow off a little steam."

Jessica insisted, "We ARE in a relationship. We have sex more times than 'now and again,'" Jessica used air quotes to emphasize her point. "I've invited you to my house. I cook for you. I've run your errands. I do everything you want. I do it for you. And, I do it gladly."

John laughed. "That's not a relationship. That's a personal assistant with benefits. I don't ask you to do anything. You volunteer. Why would I stop you from making my life easier? I'm gonna go home. You have some things to get straight in your head. If this isn't what you want, we can talk and I'll have you reassigned to a different attorney. We can end this at any point. It doesn't make any difference to me."

"You're the one getting upset. I'm asking for clarification. You can fire me if you want. That's what you mean. That would be a mistake. *I* know what you want and *I'm* the one willing to provide that for you. Who else would do that? Tell me."

"Jessie...come on. Be reasonable."

"I'm always reasonable. I am eminently reasonable. I pride myself in my reasonableness," Jessica paused. "Your wife called me *Jessie*. Why would she do that?"

"Because that's your name?"

"No, my name is Jessica. *You* call me Jessie," she felt her voice rising. "I thought that was a pet name you had for me. But, apparently, your wife uses it, too. Why is she calling me *Jessie?* Like we're friends. Like she knows something about me. About who I am. Do you talk about me at home? Do you think about me? I know you do. I can see that you do. Put any name to this 'arrangement' that you want. It's a relationship."

"I'm leaving. We'll talk about this tomorrow. I don't want to argue with you about a non-existent relationship. I work too hard to be badgered by you. I'm not sure what you want. I thought we were going to have a nice dinner. I didn't realize you were going to jump all over me. I can just go home if I want to deal with a woman who's unstable," John sighed. He stopped and looked at Jessica. "Tell me what you want and I promise to think about it. I do want you to be happy. I have to be happy, too."

"I just want an acknowledgment from you. Think about that. Think about it carefully. You can't just put me in your pocket and use me whenever it's worthwhile for you. I don't need much from you. I really don't. But, I don't want to talk to your wife and I don't want you talking to your wife about me. I think that's fair," Jessica said.

"You ask me questions about my wife all the time. I don't see why you get to talk about Alice, but she isn't allowed to ask questions about you."

"It's different."

"How?"

"I thought I was a secret. Your special secret. And now, I find out that maybe I'm not that special after all. I'm so not special that you feel comfortable introducing me to your wife," Jessica lamented.

"Again, my wife wanted to meet you. I didn't realize it was going to be that big of a deal."

"I don't want it to happen again. I don't want to watch you play the loving husband in front of my face," Jessica spat. "It's time for you to leave. I'm ready to be by myself."

"Jessie, come on. This is ridiculous."

She raised her brow. "Come on?"

"Jessie, I really don't want you reading into this. One more time, this is an arrangement that is working for me. How many different ways do you need me to explain it to you? If it isn't working for you, let me know."

"Fine. Understood. I need to think about it. I need to think about what I want," Jessica said.

"Just let me know what you decide. I'm going home to my wife."

Jessica stood in the kitchen and stirred the soup. She knew John belonged to her. He wanted her.

Alice was the problem.

*   *   *

Jessica's first real boyfriend came into her life when she was sixteen. It wasn't the boy next door, but the boy down the block. Jeff Moore. He was a varsity basketball player. Long, tall, and lean. She spent that strawberry-wine summer baking cookies for him, wearing a bikini by his pool and making out at the end of Silver Creek Road.

He wanted ice for his coke? She got ice for his coke.

He wanted her to dress pretty so they could go to the diner? She dressed pretty.

He wanted her to go to a party? She went to the party.

She enjoyed doing these things for him. He was her boyfriend. When he was happy, she was happy. It was the natural order of things.

Jessica's mother was currently dating 'Uncle' Mark. This was the first man her mother had stayed with for more than six months. Her mother nearly always started making unreasonable demands, such as forcing her boyfriend to do household chores or not cooking dinner. She consistently lost sight of how to keep a man happy. She forgot how to be accommodating. She forgot how to make sure that a man would want you.

For whatever reason, Mark had stuck around. Jessica hoped he would leave soon.

Jessica swore that she wouldn't repeat the same mistakes her mother made. Jessica would live for her boyfriend and make sure he felt appreciated. Her boyfriend would understand how much he needed her. Jeff would never leave her.

Her junior year started perfectly. She and Jeff were the 'It Couple.' That first day, she and Jeff walked hand in hand through the hallways establishing their belonging. Sitting at the large table by the cafeteria window where everyone could see them. Inviting those lucky enough to come to sit and eat with them. Snubbing those who weren't high enough in the social rankings. Reigning without crowns the way only popular kids can.

Their dynasty continued through the fall into basketball season, marred only by what Jeff called her overactive imagination. Jeff's science partner, Stacy Swansen, an attractive girl in the ordinary sense, began to constantly talk to Jeff. Every time Jessica saw him, he was speaking to Stacy.

"What's going on between you two? You're always in the library or talking in the halls. I swear one time I saw her at your house," Jessica demanded.

"Geez, Jessica. I just want to pass this class. You know I need the help. I'll fail off the team. Stacy is just helping me. Promise," Jeff said. He held up his hand and crossed his heart. He waited a moment and asked, "When did you see her at my house?"

"Nevermind. As long as you promise, promise, promise that you love me the best. And you don't care about her at all. And, you think I'm prettier."

"Promise, promise, promise," he repeated.

Mollified, Jessica walked away thinking about what dress she would buy for Homecoming. Everyone understood that she and Jeff would be named to the court. Most likely as the King and Queen. To Jessica, it only seemed right and fair.

One day after school, when the leaves started to change colors into a Halloween orange and a tarnished red, Jessica watched Jeff lightly touch the arm of another girl. Someone different from Stacy Swansen. A gangly, buck-toothed girl. She watched him speak to this girl. This ugly girl who tipped her head back and laughed at something Jeff said.

As she watched Jeff flirt with another girl, Jessica felt color start to rise to her face and her breath started coming faster. She fought to keep her composure, "Hey, Jeff. Who was that?"

"Who?"

"That girl."

"That one back there? Awww… I accidentally smacked her with my ID. I was twirling my lanyard and smacked her in the face. I was just telling her I'm sorry. It was pretty embarrassing." Jeff toed the dirt in front of him and looked down.

"I can't believe you would do that."

"I know. I'm sorry. I'll be more careful."

"What? What? You're fucking cheating on me in front of my face and you're promising me to be more careful! You asshole!"

"Uhhhhhh… Again, *I* smacked *her* in the face. It's my fault. I apologized. I'm not cheating on you."

"You are. You are such an asshole. I saw you. I literally stood right here and watched you caress her arm."

Jeff grabbed her by her shoulders and bent his knees, so he was her height. "I am looking you in the eyes. I messed up and hit her in the face. I apologized. I may have touched her arm when I made a joke. I am not cheating on you. Why are you being crazy? Seriously, why are you being crazy?"

"I don't ever want to see you again. The fact that you can do this in front of my face and then lie. I can't even look at you," Jessica was crying.

"Look. I didn't want to say anything before. I didn't want to start a fight. I'm tired of you throwing a fit every time I talk to another girl. Nothing happened. I won't keep defending myself for doing nothing. I think we're done."

Jessica took two steps back, "You're breaking up with me? Because YOU decided to talk to another girl?"

"No. I'm breaking up with you because you're crazy. Every time I talk to another girl, you lose your mind. Jessica, I'm seriously tired of it. I can't do this anymore. I don't want it to be a big deal," Jeff shrugged. "We can still be friends."

"Friends?!?! What about Homecoming? It's in three weeks," Jessica's voice rose on every word until it ended in a shriek. She clutched the front of his shirt in her hand. "You can't do this right before Homecoming. What will people think?"

"I don't care about what people think," Jeff said. "I guess we'll both be going to the dance solo."

His words were so needlessly hateful. Fucking asshole. She would show him.

She would.

*   *   *

She remembered watching his house. She watched it for at least a week. She watched as his mom came home. She watched his dad pick up his little sister's bike from the front yard. She watched the cat stroll through the picture window.

She came back the next day and she just watched.

And the day after that, she watched.

She watched until she was ready. She may not have been the most intelligent girl or the prettiest girl or even the girl that Jeff wanted, but she was the most patient. She would wait and watch until the perfect time to strike.

She knew when the family came home. She knew when they left. She knew when they woke up. She knew when they went to bed.

She knew this family.

The following Wednesday, Jessica skipped school. She didn't do it often, but she always skipped for a good reason. The last time she skipped school, Mark moved into the family home. Jessica had walked all over the neighborhood trying to process what it meant for this stranger to be living in her home. She asked her mother to throw Mark out, but Jessica's mother refused. A man would always be more important to her mother than Jessica. Her mother would never choose Jessica.

Today's school skip was to teach Jeff a lesson. To make Jeff understand how much he needed her and wanted her.

Jeff needed to understand how important she was to his life and act accordingly. She could protect him. No one else could protect him like she could. No one else knew him like she did.

She went to the back door with the spare key. Jeff always forgot his key, so the Moores kept a spare under a rock near the porch.

Letting herself into the house, Jessica singsonged, "Here, kitty, kitty, kitty. Come here, Marla. Where are yo-ou?" Jessica walked through the house looking for the cat.

She pushed open the door to Jeff's room. Knowing it to be his as she had spent many summer afternoons there. She looked around his room. A pair of sneakers carelessly thrown in front of the closet. She fingered the sweatshirt casually thrown over a desk chair. She picked it up and pulled it over her head so that she could remember Jeff's smell. To remember why she was here. In his house.

A baseball bat stood in the corner.

Likely Marla wouldn't be in Jeff's room. He hated the cat. He hated the smell of the litter box. Hated the cat hair that got all over his basketball uniforms. He put up with the cat because he adored his little sister. Adoration to a ridiculous amount, in Jessica's opinion. The death of Marla would hurt his clingy sister and convey an appropriate message to Jeff.

"Marla? Marla? Kitty, kitty, kitty." Jessica danced through the house to the music of her own voice.

She thought she heard a faint meow coming from down the hall from Jeff's parents' room. The door was open. "Marla? Come here, kitty, kitty." Marla slunk over to Jessica, winding her chubby kitty body through Jessica's legs. When

Jessica picked her up, Marla started to purr like a tiny living motor.

"Poor Marla. Poor, poor Marla," Jessica cooed.

She cradled the cat like a baby and brought it back to Jeff's bedroom. She lovingly caressed the baseball bat with the fingertips of her empty hand. Standing in the middle of his room, her mind reeled with the possibilities of what she was contemplating. Would the cat stay still?

She laid the cat on the ground and grabbed the bat with both hands. She stood with her legs about a foot apart, breathing deeply. Marla rolled onto her back. Her soft belly showed with her paws in the air. The cat looked at Jessica. Jessica raised the bat above her head and stopped.

What was she doing? This didn't make any sense.

Jessica took a deep breath and shook her head. Trying to rid her mind of these crazy thoughts.

She dropped the bat and picked up the cat, snuggling it to her chest. Marla meowed companionably.

Jessica meandered back through the house towards the kitchen. A butcher block sat quietly on the countertop. She grabbed the largest knife and she slit Marla's throat quickly and deeply before the cat even had a chance to stop purring. She dropped the blood-stained knife on the ground.

Jessica walked back to Jeff's room, kicking the dropped bat back into the corner where she had found it. She pulled the sheets and comforter down, laying Marla reverentially in the bed. Carefully pulling up the sheets and tucking the cat in.

Blood was starting to mat the cat's fur. "Poor kitty," Jessica sighed. She pet the cat's head one more time.

On her way out the door, Jessica picked up the knife and cleaned it. Sliding it back into the butcher block.

Cats could be tricky. She could have possibly missed hitting the cat with the baseball bat. Then, no lesson would have been taught.

When Jeff came home, he would understand what had happened. Killing Marla would prove Jessica's devotion to him. She would do anything for him. Maybe they would be back together by Homecoming.

Chapter Fifteen

Alice

"Hey, Natalie. I was just calling to check-in. I haven't seen you in a while and wanted to see if we could meet up for drinks sometime. I'm pretty much free all week. Let me know what works for you." Alice left the rehearsed message in the socially acceptable one breath, just under ten seconds.

She had been trying to get in touch with Natalie for weeks. Natalie's husband filed for divorce about three months ago, alleging that Natalie had engaged in numerous affairs over their eight-year marriage. The last Alice heard was that Natalie's husband was filing for sole custody of the children and refusing to pay alimony. Ryan told her this after Alice confided that Natalie wasn't taking her calls.

Natalie had apparently left the family home before she received service and the paperwork regarding the divorce. Ostensibly, to make life easier for the children.

Ryan wouldn't give her any more information.

Alice had offered up her spare bedroom in an email, but Natalie hadn't replied. Alice kept calling, but Natalie wouldn't reply. Alice sent texts, but Natalie wouldn't reply.

John looked up from his breakfast and Saturday newspaper. He and Alice sat at their dining room table, kitty-corner from each other eating the pancakes Alice had made. "Are you trying to reach Natalie again?" Alice nodded in confirmation as she pressed the end button on her cell phone. "You just need to let it go. If she wants to talk to you, she will. Maybe she's just trying to scrub everything from her old life and start over. I can imagine this whole divorce thing is hard. You might be making it harder for her by reminding her of her before life."

"Her before life? Come on. What have you been reading?" Alice scoffed.

"You're the one leaving Oprah magazine behind in the bathroom. Leave something different if you don't want me to get all in touch with my feminine side," John joked.

Alice laughed, "You are an absolute mess. Besides, I don't believe she's avoiding me because of her before life. I don't know why she's avoiding me. She needs a friend and I can be that friend for her. We haven't spoken or seen each other in forever. She still talks to Ryan, but that's not the same as staying in touch with a female friend. I keep thinking about how I would feel if I was suddenly going through a divorce."

"Well…she shouldn't have cheated on her husband. She should know better."

"What's that supposed to mean? What if it was her husband who cheated?"

John scoffed, "That's different."

"Different? How so?"

"Men and women are different. Affairs just aren't the same thing for men as they are for women. Women get *emotionally* attached. Men can separate sex from emotion. It's biology."

"I seriously can't believe you just said that."

"Said what? It is different for men."

"Oh? Did you read that in a magazine? Did Oprah clue you into that nugget of genius? Or, are you trying to tell me that you have been cheating on me our whole marriage?"

"Of course not. See, this is what I mean. You're speaking from emotion."

"You do work late a lot," Alice cocked her head and looked at John through squinted eyes. Studying him.

"Are we actually having this conversation?" John ran his fingers through his too-long hair. He was due for a haircut. Alice made a mental note to make an appointment for him later. John never remembered such things. "I'm not, nor have I ever cheated on you. Don't they say a woman always knows? Wouldn't you know in your deep, down feminine soul, if I had an affair?"

"I don't know who 'they' are, but I would hope I know you well enough now that I could tell when our marriage is in trouble."

"Our marriage is not in trouble. I'm sorry we're even having this discussion. Get in touch with Natalie if you want. But, I think she would have contacted you by now if she wanted to talk to you. Maybe it's time to let that relationship go. We need to find some new couple friends to hang out with."

"Oh, sure, we'll just find someone on the street. Run up to them and say, 'Will you be my friend?'" Alice clasped her hands together in a pleading motion and opened her eyes as large as they would go. "You work too much for us to find new friends. You aren't around. You know how hard it is for me to meet new people. I really need to hang on to the friendships that I have. For my personal sanity."

"Alice, I know it's hard for you to meet new people. I completely understand that. You know I'm around. I'm always here for you. I promise to keep my eye out for new friends. I didn't realize this friendship meant so much to you. I'll try to be home more for dinner. You know as soon as..." John stood up and moved behind Alice's chair and began to rub her soldiers.

"I know. I know. As soon as you make partner, we'll go on vacation and you'll stop working so much. I can't wait for that day to come around. I can't wait until then," Alice said.

John hugged her from behind and laid his cheek on her head, "Maybe stop trying so hard to get in touch with Natalie? People change when they go through a divorce. I know you're trying to be a good friend, but I don't want her putting crazy thoughts in your head. We're fine. Our marriage is fine. I don't want you to get more anxious and have to change your meds again. You know how hard it is to get them evened out. I just really worry about you and I want you to be okay."

"She's still my friend, John. But...I'll think about what you said."

"That's all I can ask."

*   *   *

"I'm so glad you finally got back to me," Alice reached across the table to hold her old friend's hand. Natalie looked thinner, verging on gaunt. Her roots were starting to show and Alice noticed that her usually perfectly manicured nails were bitten down to the quick.

"It's just been hard. I don't know what to say to you anymore," Natalie whispered.

"What do you mean? You can talk to me, just like always. I will always stand by you. I promise, always. Why would you do this to your family? How many affairs have you had?"

"Just one. Just…the one." Natalie took her hand back and looked down at her fingers.

"Who? Who is worth the trouble? Who is so important that you would throw away your whole life?"

Natalie looked up. "You really don't know?"

"No, I don't. John doesn't talk to your husband anymore and you haven't said anything."

"I-I have to go. I can't be here. This was a mistake. I'm so sorry, Alice. I have to go. Don't call me anymore, okay? Please. It's just easier this way." Natalie got up and left the table. Her tiny body trembling.

Alice called after her, "Natalie, what's going on? Just tell me. I can help you. Natalie. You're my best friend. I miss you. I don't care what happened. I'll understand. I won't judge you."

Natalie stopped mid-step. "You won't understand this. You won't. I don't know how it happened. It just did. I'm so sorry, Alice. I'm so sorry."

"What are you talking about? Why are you apologizing to me?"

"Goodbye. Don't contact me anymore, okay? I need to get through this on my own. I need to figure out what happened on my own. I need to live my life without you now. I need to figure out what's left of my life."

Alice watched Natalie walk out the door. She knew there was a thirty percent chance Natalie would turn around and come back. Alice waited another ten minutes until she realized one hundred percent Natalie was gone.

Chapter Sixteen

Jessica

A week after Jeff's cat died, he still hadn't approached her. Jessica waited patiently for him to acknowledge that he understood her message. But every time she saw him, he was going in a different direction or turned around a corner.

She decided to wait for him outside of the locker room after basketball practice. "Jeff! Hi! I've been looking for you."

He jumped three feet high. "Jessica. I didn't see you standing there. What are you doing here? You aren't supposed to be talking to me."

"How are we going to coordinate our outfits for Homecoming if we don't chat about it? I'm wearing a pale blue dress. You should get a tie to match. We will be the most perfect couple at the dance."

"We aren't going to Homecoming." Jeff looked around the empty hallway.

"Of course, we are. Don't be silly. You asked me this summer, don't you remember?"

"We aren't going to Homecoming together." He made a move to go back inside the locker room.

Jessica blocked his path. "Where are you going? We're still talking."

"Why is there no one else in this hallway? What happened to the rest of the guys?"

She shrugged. "I guess you took a long shower. I don't see anyone else here. It's been so hard to get a chance to talk to you. I've been waiting for a few days."

"I'm not supposed to be alone with you."

"What? Why?"

"You're insane. You're seriously insane. Go away, Jessica. Don't talk to me." She felt movement behind her. "Coach! Coach!" Jeff yelled over her shoulder.

She could hear footsteps coming up behind her. Turning around, Jessica saw the basketball coach, who doubled as a science teacher, approaching. "Jessica, what are you doing here? Are you even supposed to be in school?"

"What are you talking about, Mr. Lawson? Where else would I be?"

"I just thought… Anyway, you aren't supposed to be within one hundred feet of Jeff. The principal put out a memo. Jessica, you *know* that. Don't make me call the resource officer. The principal asked us to report to her if we saw you anywhere on school grounds. I don't really want to have to do that. Why don't you just go home?" Mr. Lawson said.

"Oh. My. God. Jeff, did you do this? Did you call the police or something?"

"My parents called the police. What did you think was going to happen? There's something extremely wrong with you," Jeff said, inching away from her along the school's concrete wall.

"I was just trying to show you that we belong together. I thought you would get the hint. I know you didn't mean to break up with me and I forgive you," Jessica stated.

"You fucking killed my sister's cat," Jeff spat.

"I didn't do it. Besides, it's just an animal."

"Yes, you did. You know you did! You broke into my house! You were in my fucking bedroom. You are a fucking psychopath. Stay away from me and stay away from my family." Jeff brought himself up to his full height and pushed his shoulder into her body as he walked past her. Jessica fell into the wall smacking her head on it.

"Jessica, I think it's time for you to go," Coach Lawson said.

"Did you see that? Did you see what he did? Jeff, you can't treat me this way! You can't just push me away! I would never do anything to hurt you! You know that! Please, Jeff. Just come back and let's talk about." She watched Jeff keep walking away from her. Jessica started sobbing. She fell to her knees in front of a locker room with smells of sweat and unclean bodies pouring out of it. "Jeff, this isn't over. It's not over! I won't let it be over."

Jeff never stopped walking.

He never looked back.

"Jessica, it's time to go," Coach Lawson stated again. He gingerly took her elbow with two fingers. "Come with me. Now."

She allowed Coach to escort her to the principal's office. She gave no resistance. She wondered if her life was over.

"Jessica, please come into my office," the principal commanded. She pointed to a chair for Jessica to sit in. Jessica sat. "What are you doing here? We sent a letter to your home stating that for the time being you are suspended from school. We can't have students physically harming other students. We won't put up with it. I won't put up with it," the principal droned on. Blah. Blah. Blah. "Do you have anything that you want to say?"

"Not really," Jessica answered.

"Go outside and sit on the bench. I've called your mother."

"Awesome. It doesn't matter. She doesn't care about me. I'll go wait like a good girl. That's what everyone wants me to do. Be a good girl. Just say it."

The principal just pointed towards the door.

Her mom showed up thirty minutes later, looking harried and rushed. Her ordinarily perfect attire wrinkled. "I'm sorry. I was in the middle of prepping dinner for my family. I didn't hear my phone ring," her mom rushed to explain.

"It's fine, but, Mrs. Allen, I need to talk to you about your daughter."

"Please don't call me Mrs. Allen. I haven't been Mrs. Allen for a very long time."

The principal made a no matter gesture with her hands and ushered her mom inside the office and closed the door. She stayed inside for about twenty minutes.

When her mom came out, she just stared at Jessica and held up one finger, "Don't speak to me right now. Just…don't. I need to calm down."

"Mom, I…"

"Jessica, not now. I need to discuss some things with Mark."

"What are you going to discuss with Uncle Mark? Is he just going to come riding in on a white horse and save the day?"

"Don't be smart. I need to figure out where you're going to go to school because you're done here. The fact that you flat out lied to Mark and me about the incident at Jeff's. You said his mom was exaggerating on the phone. That you didn't do anything," her mom stopped. She waited a few minutes and steadied herself, "But mostly, but mostly… it's the fact that I don't even know who you are anymore. The fact that you scare me, Jessica. You are scaring me and I don't know how to help you." Her mom started to cry.

"Don't cry, mom. There's nothing to cry about. Jeff and I had a little fight and I was trying to make it up to him in the best way that I knew how."

Her mom just looked at her, "By killing a cat? In what world does that even make sense?" she paused. "Are you even sorry, Jessica? Do you even care? Please tell me that much. Convince me that you care. How did we not know about the restraining order?"

"First, I didn't do anything wrong. I really didn't. I just went to visit Jeff because we broke up. Everyone is making a much bigger deal out of this than it is, I swear," Jessica said. "They served the restraining order when you and Mark were out at dinner. I decided not to tell you about it. I didn't want you to be mad."

"I don't know how to fix you. I really don't. You've had problems for so long. They just keep getting worse. Mark and I want to get married and have a baby, but I worry so much. You seem to be losing all sense of reality. All sense of right and wrong."

"What are you worried about? Have a baby. Nobody cares."

"Jessica, remember when you used to babysit for the Thompkins and then they told you to not come around anymore? They told me that you had dropped the baby. They said they had to take him to the emergency room. I didn't believe you could do something like that on purpose. I figured it had to be an accident."

"Good. Because I didn't do that."

"Then your friend Jane. You wouldn't go an hour without speaking to her. You two were joined at the hip. She doesn't come around anymore. I asked her what had happened. She said everything was fine, but she wouldn't look me in the eye. I still don't know what happened."

"Mom, you can't trust Jane. She always liked to tell stories," Jessica sighed. "We were just playing a game and she got a little hurt."

"Her mother told me Jane received thirty stitches. That's not a little hurt. She told me that right before she asked for you to never come to their house again. I almost moved because I was so ashamed of you," her mom said. "And now this. Jessica, I can't have another baby right now, because I'm so afraid of what you will do. I can't watch you all the time. I just can't."

"Grow up, Mom. Everyone is overreacting. You're overreacting. Have a baby with Uncle Mark. See if I care. Personally, I think you should be more worried about having him around a new baby than worried about what I might do.

Hopefully, it won't be a girl," Jessica lashed out. Mark had never touched her, but it would do her mom good to think that the Great Mark had some nasty streaks.

"What are you trying to say?"

"I'm not trying to say anything. I've said it before about my 'uncles,' you just don't want to listen," Jessica said.

Jessica's mom slapped her across the face. "Don't be disgusting. I can't deal with this anymore."

The corners of Jessica's mouth tipped up slightly and she laughed softly as if to herself. "By this, you mean me. That you can't deal with me anymore. Guess what, mom. You've never dealt with me. You just go away with whatever boyfriend you have at the time and you never care about me. You're never interested in me or what I have to say. I'm not important."

"You know that's not true. You make things so difficult. So difficult. I hope Mark can help."

"Oh, I'm sure he can help. Do you even like him, or is it his money that you like?"

"I can't speak to you when you're like this," her mom said. "We're going home. I need you to go straight to your room when we get there. I'll let you know when we're ready to have an adult conversation about your future."

"Cool. Whatever. Fine. I definitely shouldn't be included in any kind of conversation about my future until you and Mark figure it out," Jessica snapped.

*   *   *

"Jessica, this is a very serious matter. You need to go to school. Due to your behavioral issues, only a reform school will admit you. Your mother and I have discussed this matter at length. And, you should know, we have discussed it previous to the current incident," Mark stated.

"Whatever," Jessica replied. She sat on the couch with the coffee table in front of her. Her mother and Mark had pulled up kitchen chairs and sat across from her, mimicking a police interrogation room.

"That's exactly the problem. I have told your mother over and over again that she's too lenient with you. That you have special problems and need to attend a school that can handle special teenagers like you," Mark continued as if he had never been interrupted.

He spread some pamphlets out on the table. "I've been collecting these for a few years. I think, and your mother agrees, that you need to go to a boarding school. We can't keep track of you anymore. Your mother and I want to start a family and you have been very disruptive towards that endeavor."

"I get it. You just want me out of the house. I'm not part of your perfect family," Jessica said.

Her mom interjected, "Jessica, you know that's not true. Your...your problems are just becoming too much for us to handle. We need to send you to professionals. To people who can help you. Maybe, some medication would..."

"Medication!" Jessica screeched. "You want to dope me up! You're a great mom. Just great. First, you smack me in the face today. Now, you want to send me to somewhere that will just medicate your problem away. What will your friends say about that? You know they are going to talk about you behind your back. What are you going to do then? No one will think you have a perfect family."

"Jessica, don't speak to your mother in that manner. This has been a challenging situation for her. For both of us, really.

You aren't helping." Mark picked up a particular pamphlet. "This school is in Ohio and it specializes in children with behavioral and developmental issues. Please pack a suitcase. I've contacted the headmistress. She expects you tomorrow."

"Tomorrow?!? Don't I have a say in this at all?"

"No, dear, you don't. It's been decided," Mark said.

"Fuck you! I fucking hate you. Mom, don't let him do this to me. Please. Don't send me away. I'm sorry for everything. I love you. Please don't send me away. I promise I'll be better. I'll be so much better."

Her mom whispered, "I agree with Mark. Don't make this more difficult than it has to be."

"I won't go. I'll run away."

Mark sighed and looked at her mom. "I told you this was going to happen. We should have just packed the suitcase for her and dropped her off."

"You can't make me go. I won't go. You don't own me."

"Give me one second," Mark said. He left the room and she could hear him murmuring into his cell phone.

"Mom, please don't do this. I know this isn't what you want."

"Jessica, the thing is, I don't know what else to do," her mom explained through tears falling down her face like a waterfall. "I hope this school can fix you. I want you to have a wonderfully normal life. To find people to love. To find people who love you back."

"Don't you love me?" Jessica asked.

Her mom waited for several beats before answering. "I just don't know anymore. I'm sorry. I just don't know."

Mark came back into the room. "Can we at least have one more nice family dinner?"

"Fuck you!" Jessica screamed and ran to her room. She slammed the door and began to throw clothes into her backpack. She wouldn't let them send her away. She would just leave of her own volition. They would never see her again.

She heard the front door opening and voices in the foyer. She listened to steps in the hallway with the same murmur of voices. She watched her door open.

"This is for the best. For you and for us. I hope this helps," Mark said. "Don't make this harder than it needs to be."

Jessica saw two large men behind him. "What are you doing? What are you trying to do?"

"Gentlemen, this is Jessica. Please take her to school."

Jessica screamed and spat and arched her back, not unlike a feral cat. In the end, they took her to boarding school. She stayed there for the next two years.

She didn't come back when her mom and Mark married.

She didn't come back when the baby was born.

She came back when it was time to teach them a lesson.

Chapter Seventeen

Detective Morrison

Morrison knocked on an average-looking door in an average-looking apartment complex. He had knocked on far too many of these doors throughout his career. He instinctively stood to the side with one hand on his service weapon. A person looking through the peephole wouldn't be able to see him and he could react quickly, if need be.

He thought back to when standing this way hadn't been quite as ingrained. He remembered approaching these universal doors full-on, chest first. The first time he served a subpoena, his training officer pushed him to the side. "What are you doing? Are you trying to get killed? You don't know who is on the other side of the door," his training officer screamed at him. It was a lesson Morrison never forgot.

A middle-aged woman opened the door. Pretty, except she was far too thin. She had a lean look around her eyes, as if she needed to decide soon whether she was going to give up on life or keep fighting. "Can I help you?"

"Natalie McInroe?"

"Yes."

Morrison held up his badge. "I'm Detective Morrison. Can I ask you a few questions?"

"About what?"

"Do you know a John Smith?"

"Yes," McInroe answered.

"Can I come in?"

"Do I need a lawyer?"

"Do you think you need a lawyer?"

"Maybe."

Morrison looked McInroe over. "Why don't you come down to the station where we can talk? You can call a lawyer if you want. I think you know what this is about."

"Let me grab my coat. I can drive myself. Just give me the address."

"Yes, ma'am." Morrison decided to trust her to show up. No actual harm done if she didn't. It was only a simple vandalism charge.

Morrison drove to the station. He waited outside on a bench for McInroe to park and walk over. He held the door open for her as they entered. "Follow me. We'll just go over to my desk. I have a Miranda form that I need you to initial, while I read it to you. Do you want to call your lawyer?"

"I don't have any money. My husband and I split up. He won't give me any more money. I've tried to get help from some other people, but it's taking everything I have and more right now just to pay for food and the apartment."

Morrison lead McInroe through the station trying to ignore her statements. "Here's the form. It's your basic Miranda form. I'm going to read it to you. I just need you to initial each statement. This first one states that you have the right to remain silent," he said.

McInroe initialed it.

"Anything you say can and will be used against you in a court of law." McInroe initialed. "You have the right to an attorney. If you can't afford an attorney, one will be provided for you." McInroe initialed. "Do you understand these rights as I've read them to you?"

"Yes, I do. I don't want an attorney. I just want this to be over."

"Ms. McInroe, I have video of you throwing paint and breaking windows on John Smith's car."

"You have video?"

"A very clear security video," Morrison lied easily.

"Oh."

"Do you want to tell me what happened?"

"I was so angry. He destroyed my whole life and nothing happened to him. Nothing. He probably just went on to a different girl. Alice was my best friend. I betrayed her. I betrayed my husband. For what? For that piece of shit? Something should happen to him. Not just to me. To him."

"To be clear, the 'he' in question is John Smith? And you had an affair with him?" Morrison asked.

"Yes, to both," McInroe answered softly, not meeting Morrison's eyes.

"So, you destroyed his car?"

"He loves that fucking car. Thinks it's a status symbol. He didn't even buy it. Alice's parents bought it for him as a gift," McInroe said. "At first, I was only going to key his car. Somehow it just morphed into something more. Am I going to go to jail?"

"I have strong doubts that Mr. Smith will prosecute, but I have to call him and tell him what's going on. This whole horrible, yucky situation. I'm making it worse."

"I can't pay for it. I know I did it, but I can't pay for it. I shouldn't have done it. I'm just making everything worse."

Morrison felt stirrings of pity towards the woman. Certainly, he had better things to do than pursue a charge against a woman who just gave a dirtbag a little piece of his own shit to eat. "Please give me your phone number. I will get in touch with Mr. Smith and see what he wants to do. Does his wife know that you were having an affair with him?" Morrison pulled out a post-it note and passed it to Natalie.

"No! I'm not having an affair anymore. I don't want him to touch me!" she paused. "I didn't tell her. I don't think he told her either. I can't tell her. I've tried. I'm a horrible person," she began to cry.

Morrison ignored the tears with practiced ability, "Your ace in the hole is the wife doesn't know about the affair. I'll see if I can help you smooth this over with Smith. He might be willing to drop all charges."

"Why would you help me? I'm a criminal."

Morrison chuckled. "You're hardly a criminal. I'll never say that someone deserves to be a victim. But if there's an asshole in the world who deserves it, it's this guy."

"Thank you," McInroe said. "What else do you need from me?"

"I need to make sure you don't leave the city. I don't want to have to track you down again."

"I don't have any money to go anywhere. My husband has taken everything from me. Everything."

"I understand, except I'm pretty sure it was my wife that won my divorce. There's a lot of people who will understand. Don't hold it against yourself forever. Also, please write down a good phone number." Ms. McInroe began to jot down her number on the post-it note she had been handed. He continued, "I will call Mr. Smith and get back to you as soon as I understand his position on formally filing a complaint and informing his wife of the culprit and said culprit's motivation."

Chapter Eighteen

Alice

"Detective Morrison. I assume you have finally figured out who vandalized my car?" Alice overheard John speaking into the phone from her position in the kitchen. "Yes. Mm-hmm. And you would have to do that? No, I don't understand. Well, who is going to pay for the damages?"

Alice waved her wine glass at him. "Did they find out who did it?" she mouthed. John quickly shushed her and stepped out onto the balcony sliding the door shut behind him. Alice turned back to the stove to finish sauteing the vegetables for dinner.

Through the transparent door, she watched him run his fingers through his hair. He still needed a haircut and she had forgotten to make the appointment. She thought he formed the words, "Fine. Fine. If that's the way it has to be."

John stayed out on the balcony for a few more minutes. "Hey, babe. Sorry about that. That was the detective. He says they don't have any leads on my car. The security camera wasn't working and they couldn't find anyone who saw something. I really didn't expect much from them. Look what happened at the station. It was amateur hour."

"Groan. Well, I've already called the insurance company and started the paperwork. Will I just have them send the check directly to the body shop? I'll see if I can get a final copy of the police report. I'm sure the insurance will want to see it, before they payout," Alice said.

"You do so much for me. Why don't you let me take this over? It's my car, after all. I appreciate that you started the process when I was so upset, but I'll do it," John said.

"Are you sure? I really don't mind. All that's left is forwarding a copy of the report and a quick phone call to confirm everything," Alice replied.

"I'm so sure. You did the hard part. I just asked for the report over the phone. I still have to put in a request, but I can pick it up in a couple of days when it's finished. They're going to charge a dollar a page, which is ridiculous, but that's bureaucracy."

"I won't stop you. You should report the security company to the partners. They charge fifteen thousand a month for office space. The property management company should be providing all of the services that you pay for."

"Absolutely," John agreed. He opened the cabinet containing their dinner plates. "I'll set the table, while you finish up the rest."

"That's fair," she kissed him on the bridge of his nose.

Alice observed John throughout dinner. It was unusual for him to volunteer to do any type of duty that he considered a 'domestic errand.' Calling the insurance company or picking up a police report both certainly counted in this category. Throughout their marriage, he had always left these mundane tasks to her. He never wanted to be bothered with them.

Spearing her chicken with her fork, Alice asked, "John, is there something you aren't telling me? You were so upset when this happened. And... now it feels like you're just trying to brush it away."

"I'm not brushing it away, but they don't know who vandalized the car. There's no reason to belabor the point. I just spoke to the police officer. I'll just finish up with the insurance company. I don't understand why you are fighting so hard to take care of this. I'm just trying to help you out. I know that sometimes I leave a lot of our daily lives to you and it must be hard."

"I'm not trying to fight you about it. It's just not something that you usually do and I'm confused as to your motivations. The whole thing just feels strange to me."

"Confused as to my motivations? Who talks like that?" He smiled and reached for her hand. "I guess I'm just being a good husband. Do you think that's possible?"

Alice smiled, "Yeah, I guess that's possible."

Chapter Nineteen

Jessica

essica prided herself on being introspective and having the ability to critique herself honestly. Not many people could do that. Most people lived their whole lives not ever looking inward to solve their problems. These people always looked towards the world or their interactions with other people to explain their faults or reactions.

Not Jessica.

She never forgot her mom or Jeff claiming that she was a psychopath. Words like that could stay with a person for a very long time. Influence their later behavior, if a person allowed them.

She memorized the definition for psychopath: A person with an egocentric or antisocial personality marked by a lack of remorse for one's actions or empathy for others. She had pondered this definition at length for years. She took it apart, looking at every word and seeing if it applied to her.

Was she egocentric? Absolutely not. She wasn't very concerned with herself. Certainly not to the point that she raised her own needs above others. She believed in acts of charity. Of giving to those supposedly in need. She felt most needs existed for people to receive attention instead of being actually in "need." However, being seen as charitable was an essential facet in normal society. Jessica understood that.

She didn't believe that she was anti-social. She actively sought out the company of men who interested her. Men who wanted to spend time with her. True, she didn't have many (or any at all) female friends. Women tended to be difficult, emotional creatures. Jessica found them irritating and, generally, lacking in intellect.

So, no anti-social tendencies could be attributed to her.

Any claims of lack of remorse were blatantly untrue. She did feel bad about her actions. She wished people didn't force her to the limit. To teach them difficult lessons. It took an exceptional person to be able to teach specific lessons. To be able to accept the consequences that may come from teaching.

The final portion of the definition required a lack of empathy. Empathy meant being aware of and understanding the feelings of other people. This part of the definition caused Jessica the most struggle. She was aware of other people's feelings and could generally understand why they felt a certain way. She just didn't care. That seemed to be the actual point of the term "lack of empathy." Did lacking one portion of an extensive definition qualify her as a psychopath?

For example, what about Avery Downing? He was a mistake. Not the first mistake Jessica had ever made in her life. But, a mistake. A huge mistake. A mistake that forced her to move across the country. When she thought about whether or not she was a psychopath, she always thought about Avery.

*   *   *

Five years ago

"Hi! I'm new here. I'm already late for my new job and I know it's not very manly to ask for directions, but I need directions. I don't have any idea where I'm supposed to be going. Please help me to not get fired on my first day. Please. Please. You look like an angel. Tell me you're an angel and that you can help me."

Jessica laughed. The man standing in front of her had just graduated from law school eagerness, warm brown eyes and beautiful caramel skin. "I'm not an angel, but I think I can help. What law firm are you going to?"

"What gave it away?"

"The brand-new business case without any scratches or scuffs on it."

Avery toed the floor and smiled sheepishly. "I guess you caught me. Which floor is Scranton and Duff?"

"They have the top six floors. Go to floor thirty-four and there should be a receptionist sitting there who can help you."

"You are an angel. Never say that you aren't again. I'll see you soon," Avery blew her a kiss. Jessica noticed a wedding band on his finger as he waived to her from the elevator.

At the time, she worked for the property management company that owned the building and directed people to various floors, as necessary. She qualified for the position by being pretty, quiet and able to show up on time. She spent most of the day whiling away her hours on Facebook or some other social media platform. The job wasn't challenging. It paid all right, though. Jessica figured a man would eventually supply the rest of the money that she needed.

Avery came into the building every day around the same time. Every day they exchanged some sort of banter. He wasn't the only man Jessica was friendly with or the only man she was watching. But, she desired him the most.

At the end of the week, Avery set a coffee cup down on her desk. "I just want to officially introduce myself now, since it looks like I won't be fired immediately. I'm Avery Downing. I think you're cute and I brought you some hot chocolate."

"Not coffee?"

"Not everyone drinks coffee, but everyone drinks hot chocolate."

"That's true," Jessica smiled. "I'm Jessica Allen."

"I figured your name wasn't 'receptionist' as it says there on your super fancy plaque."

Jessica laughed appropriately.

From that day forward, Avery stopped by her desk every day before he entered the elevator for his floor. He stopped to make a joke or compliment her before he went home. Eventually, he invited her to drinks.

Eventually, he invited her to dinner.

Eventually, he invited her to a small condo around the corner from the building.

"The firm owns a few of these condos and we use them for housing witnesses or having parties or whatever we need them for," Avery said as he opened the door.

"It's stunning. What do you plan on using it for?" Jessica asked.

Avery pulled her to his body and pushed her against the door. Letting his hands roam free as his mouth devoured her.

"Oh, I see," Jessica said when they broke apart.

They spent the night together in that beige-washed apartment. In the morning, she asked Avery about his wife.

He pulled on his pants and turned away from Jessica. "I don't want her to be a part of this. I need something that is just mine. Can you be mine? Just mine? I'll take care of you. I promise."

Jessica consented.

And then, Avery did take care of her. He took her to restaurants and plays. He bought her skimpy lingerie. He constantly doted on her. Giving her everything she could possibly want.

Until, he didn't.

*   *   *

Jessica sat on the couch in the condo and watched dispassionately as Avery entered with his new mistress.

"Hello. I wondered how long it would take you to get to this point. I've been checking the housing schedule for a few weeks waiting for you to reserve it. Did you know that I updated it for your firm? It's sort of a side project I volunteered for," Jessica called out.

The new mistress screamed.

"What are you doing here? How did you get here?" Avery asked.

"It's a very long, not interesting story. What's important is that I'm here now," Jessica answered.

His new mistress stood to the side gasping like a trout, holding her hands to her heart. "You aren't supposed to be here," she finally managed.

"I would say that you aren't supposed to be here either, but I guess that isn't true," Jessica shrugged. "You know, since this is the place where you bring mistresses, so the wives don't find out."

"I'm not a mistress!" she yelled out.

"Aren't you, though?" Jessica asked.

"Can we address the fact that you aren't supposed to be here?" Avery asked. He still seemed to be trying to exert authority in a situation in which he had none.

"I visited this apartment with Gregory Wayne just last week. We had a lovely time. He has excellent taste in food and wine. Finishes ever so quickly and then just falls asleep. He's quite the dear."

"I don't understand. Why were you here with a senior partner? What are you doing behind my back?" Avery questioned.

"I still don't understand why she's here," the new mistress murmured.

Jessica looked at Avery. "She is very stupid. Does that bother you at all? Yes. I was here with a senior partner. Does it bother you more that I was here with a senior partner or would it bother you if I visited with anyone? Is it the status of the person or the fact that it's someone else that matters? I'm just curious."

"I don't know how to deal with this right now. Can you please leave?"

Jessica held up the key to the apartment. "Why? I have a key. I took an impression from the key Gregory had while he was taking his little snooze. I have as much right to be here as she does. Maybe, more."

The mistress crossed her arms in front of her. She pouted towards Avery, "Can you please make her leave? I'm tired of her."

Avery looked wholly bewildered. "Jessica, what do you want from me? I thought we had an understanding. We had a little fun. Now, I'm having a little fun with someone else. You are, too."

"I wasn't having fun. It was a means to an end. You can't treat people any way you want to and cast them aside when you're done with them. People would call that having a lack of empathy. Do you lack empathy, Avery?" Jessica pulled a small pink .380 with a silencer attached from her purse and pointed it at him.

"Where did you get that? Ohmigod! Where did you get that? What are you doing?" Avery rushed all of the words, so they all sounded as if they were one word.

At the same time, the mistress started to scream.

"MAKE HER SHUT UP!" Jessica yelled.

The mistress did not.

Jessica turned up the music and shot three times from a distance of about ten feet. The mistress was hit once in the lungs, once in the arm and once in the stomach. She didn't die right away, but she stopped screaming. Jessica felt good about that.

"Avery, come sit over here on the couch with me. I want to talk this through."

Avery looked stunned. The whites of his eyes too large in contrast to his pupils. His whole body had started to shake.

"I can't believe you did that. What kind of monster are you?"

"I'm not a monster at all. Not at all. She made me shoot her. I didn't have a choice. She wouldn't SHUT UP," Jessica paused. "You're the monster. You understand that, don't you?" Jessica pointed the gun at Avery for emphasis.

There was a knock at the door. "It's the superintendent! Is everything ok in there?"

Jessica went to sit down. "Get rid of him," she commanded. "Don't do anything crazy. I mean it. Please don't make me do something that I don't want to do."

The mistress on the bloody floor gurgled lightly in agreement.

Avery slowly opened the door and used his body to block the super's view. "Hi, sir. Everything is ok."

"Some tenants reported hearing a female screaming. You don't mind if I check and see if there's a woman here," the super said.

"Oh my gosh! That was probably me." Jessica walked into the super's view, resting the gun in the small of Avery's back. "He was trying to tickle me and I threatened him that I would scream. You know how it can get. I'm so sorry. I'll be quieter. Please forgive me." The top four buttons of her blouse were open to reveal a lacy black bra underneath. Her breasts nearly spilled out the top.

Blushing, the super nodded. "Well, just keep it down, ok?"

Jessica smiled and blew him a kiss. Avery shut the door quietly behind the man.

"Go sit on the couch. We need to talk about our future. I'm not sure where this relationship is headed right now," Jessica directed.

"What exactly is it that you want to talk about?"

"Well…us. What are you doing here with her? I thought we had something going," Jessica said.

"Are you going to kill me?"

"Yes. Yes, I think so. It isn't that hard to kill people. Everyone wants it to be hard. They want it to feel hard. But, it's not. Not really."

"Have you killed people before?"

"Yes."

"You're a psychopath."

"That word again. I hate that word. People have called me that word my whole life. It's so rude. It's a word that people call you when they don't think you're a human being. Do you think that? Think that I'm a psychopath."

Avery shifted uncomfortably on the couch. Tears stained his face. "If you let me go, I won't say anything."

"Of course, you will. You won't be able to help it. You're too scared to *not* tell anyone. You aren't the kind of man that I can trust with a secret," Jessica said sadly. She traced the trail of his tears with the tip of the gun. "I understand that you're flawed. I wish I had seen it earlier. Don't be sad about it. This is more of an 'it's not you, it's me' conversation. I shouldn't have expected so much."

"What did you expect from me?" Avery whispered.

"I expected you to at least give me the decency of breaking up with me. Instead, you snuck around behind my back. What happened? Should I have cooked more? Did I insult you in some way? I really thought this was working. Is there something wrong with me?" She took off the rest of her blouse and began to caress his face with the barrel of the gun.

"My wife is pregnant," Avery blurted.

"I doubt that. I doubt that very much. Even if that's true, you obviously don't care." Jessica motioned to the now dead woman on the floor.

"I'll do anything. I'll give you anything you want."

"You won't even answer my questions."

"I will. I will answer them completely," Avery started to blabber.

"I'm trying to understand why men constantly cheat on me. They always seem to like me at first, but then... This always happens."

"Please. Please. Don't hurt me," Avery began to breathe in and out very quickly.

"Answer the question," Jessica stopped caressing his face and jammed the gun into his cheek.

"Please. You...You...You're too easy. You're a good time girl," Avery squeaked.

Jessica shot him in the face. The silencer again muffled the sound of the shot. "Wrong. Wrong answer."

She looked around the apartment. At the mistress' body on the floor. At Avery's body slumped on the couch.

Jessica put the gun back in her purse. She tied the scarf over her head and put on her sunglasses. She would have to move to a new city now. It was such a pain when things like this happened.

She supposed the super would recognize her. But, she looked like a million other young, blonde women who chased successful men. Her fingerprints would be all over the apartment, but she didn't have any prints on file with any law enforcement agency. Also, this was a mistress apartment. Many young women who looked similar to her would have their prints here.

That said, it was likely time to move on. To a new city.
To find a new man.
The right man.

Chapter Twenty

Alice

"Should I try and talk to Natalie again?" Alice sat on the living room couch next to John as flicked through TV stations.

"Why? I thought she made her feelings very clear when she left you at lunch. Pretty sure she doesn't want to be friends anymore," John responded.

"I just feel like there is more to the story. It's just so not like her. It's so strange. She thought I knew who she had an affair with. She didn't outright say it. But she was shocked that I didn't know. How would I know? She hasn't spoken to me in months. Ryan might know, but he hasn't said anything to me."

John finally settled on a conservative cable news station and set down the remote. "I think you're reading too much into this. Why don't you just let it be? Maybe she just doesn't want to be friends anymore."

"She looks so bad. You might not even recognize her. Maybe, I'll just invite her to drinks. That should be easier for her. More of a quick catch-up between friends than a full dinner. Drinks are at least eighty percent cheaper than a full dinner anyway. I really want her to know that I'm on her side," Alice said earnestly.

"Babe, just leave her alone."

Alice ignored John's advice and sent Natalie a text: *R U OK? Drinks 2moro? 6 pm at our fav bar?*

It pinged a half-second later. She stared at the message on the screen: "Your text messages will go through, as usual. They just won't be delivered to the user."

"John, look at this message. What does that even mean?"

"It looks like someone blocked you. Were you trying to reach Natalie?"

"Yeah. I've been trying to call her all day, but it just rings and rings. I thought maybe a text would work."

"Natalie sent you a clear sign to leave her alone. She's sent a few. I hope you receive it this time."

Alice stood up suddenly and grabbed her coat.

John looked alarmed. "Where are you going?"

"To Natalie's new apartment."

"I don't think that's a good idea. How do you even know where she lives now?"

"I sent Ryan a message. He's still in touch with her. He's been to her apartment apparently and said it wasn't in a very nice neighborhood."

"She should be happy that she has somewhere to live," John said. He changed the channel again and continued, "Babe, think this through. She doesn't want to talk to you."

"Well, I'm not giving her that choice. I don't give up on my friends. Especially when I know they need me. I've asked Ryan for her address. I'm going."

John stood up and grabbed his wallet and keys. "I'm not letting you go alone."

"I'll be fine. I'm sure I'm overreacting."

"Sometimes, when people are on the precipice, you don't know what can happen. I don't want you to be alone. I don't trust her. Her whole life has fallen apart. She's not the same person that you knew," John explained. "You aren't doing this alone. That's final."

Alice hugged him. "Thank you for always being there for me. I don't think you need to come, but it means a lot to me that you want to."

She and John drove the thirty minutes to Natalie's apartment in relative silence. The wealthy suburbs slowly gave way to smaller cottages. Ultimately, giving way to industrial-looking apartment buildings as they drove deeper into the city's neighborhoods. "Kind of a step down from living right down the street from us, isn't it?"

"John, don't be so judgmental," Alice admonished.

"I'm not being judgmental. I'm just making a statement. Maybe next time she'll take better care of her marriage." He took his non-driving hand and massaged the back of Alice's neck. "Maybe this will let her know what's important in life."

"Well...now you're being nice, but still judgmental. We don't know what was going on in her marriage. Maybe she was unhappy."

"Or bored," John said.

"I don't know what to do with you," Alice responded. "You don't end your marriage because you're bored."

"Sure, you do."

Alice looked askance at John. "Should I be worried?"

"You never have to worry about me. I will never leave you. How many times do we have to talk about this before you believe me? I don't want to keep rehashing this same conversation for the rest of our lives," John commented.

"Oh, John. Don't be angry. This whole thing is just really hard for me. It's just making me question things that I would never have thought of before," Alice said.

"Let's just get this finished with, so you can close the door on your relationship with Natalie and feel okay about it," John said.

They pulled into an apartment complex about five stories tall. The grounds were relatively well-kept, but showed signs of age. There were clumps of weeds pushing up through the sidewalk. The immediate foyer looked like it had last been remodeled ten years ago. "This isn't too bad," Alice remarked. "Let's go see Natalie."

They walked into the building. Alice noticed that there wasn't a doorman or a buzzer to let them in. The lobby smelled faintly of urine. They walked straight onto the elevator with no questions asked and stepped out onto Natalie's floor without so much as a whimper.

Alice rapped on Natalie's door. No one answered. She checked her watch and sighed. It was nine p.m. Too late to be making a house call, but they were already on her doorstep.

Alice knocked again. Again, nothing.

John made a fist and pounded on the door. "Natalie, open up the damn door. Alice wants to talk to you."

Natalie opened the door an inch, only far enough to see part of John's face. "What are *you* doing here?"

"I wanted to make sure that you're ok. I'm so worried about you," Alice responded.

"You both came together. You came with Alice?" Natalie asked.

"Can we come in?" Alice asked.

"What the actual fuck is wrong with you? I'm done. I am done. Don't come around here anymore. Don't call me. Don't text me. I swear to God, I am four seconds away from calling the police. You are destroying my life!" Natalie spat.

"I'm just trying to help you. I just want to help," Alice finished lamely.

"Stop it. Just stop it. Fuck you. I wish I had never met you. I wish I had never spoken to you." Natalie closed the door. She screamed through the door, "Leave you fucking asshole! Fucking leave."

Alice fell back against the hallway wall as if she had been physically pushed. She slid against the wall down to the ground. Her hand covered her mouth. "Why does she hate me so much? I just want to help. I don't understand."

"Sometimes, people don't want your help. Sometimes you just can't help them. This is proof. You have been nothing but a sweetheart to her and she slammed the door in your face." John picked Alice up off the floor. "Don't talk to her again. I don't like seeing you this upset. Come on. I'll take us home."

Alice allowed John to lead her back to her car. She sat in the passenger seat and pressed her face against the cool window. "I don't understand what's happening. Why is she being so cruel? I never, ever tried to hurt her. Never. Zero times," Alice began to softly cry.

John began to pet her hair. "Please, don't contact her again. Please, don't. This hurts me so much. To see you like this. I'll get you home as soon as I can."

Alice cried the entire way. She cried during the traffic stop where John received a speeding ticket. She cried while she answered the officer's questions. She cried when John carried her out of the car into the house. She cried as John undressed her and laid her on the bed. She cried until she fell asleep.

At two in the morning, Alice sat straight up in bed. Eyes swollen. Tear tracks down her face. She turned and looked at her husband, who still slept next to her. She realized what she hadn't seen before. Natalie hadn't said a word to her.

Not one word.

She had spoken only to John.

Chapter Twenty-one

Natalie

"What are you doing here again? Why can't you just move on? I told you not to come back here. Didn't you do enough damage last time you showed up? Last time, the senior partner called me into his office and told me to keep my dick in my pants," John hissed at her.

Natalie walked into John's pristine office with everything in its place. She noted the perfect assistant sitting outside with perfect hair and perfect clothing. She stood in front of John, bowing slightly at the middle, trying to placate him.

"You need to give me some money. I quit my job. I couldn't look at Alice anymore. I couldn't talk to her. My husband threw me out of the house. I don't even get to see my kids. This is your fault. You need to fix it," Natalie pleaded.

"My fault? I gave you the heads up that would happen. I don't know why you didn't believe me. You've lost your mind. Last time I checked, you were enjoying yourself. Remember I pressed you up against the wall and..."

"I could tell Alice. I could tell Alice everything."

John lifted an eyebrow. "Really? You've made that threat once and you didn't go through with it. I doubt that you would say anything now. How would that conversation go? Let me think. Something like this: 'Hey, Alice. Just wanted to let you know that I've been fucking your husband for the last six months. Since we're best friends and everything, would you like to compare notes?'"

"Don't be disgusting."

John laughed, "I'm just really curious how that conversation would go. Give me the details. I'm ready."

"I'll do it. I promise I will. I'll tell her."

"I don't think you will. I don't think you want her to know about this horrible part of you. You just like to talk a lot. You had the option yesterday and you didn't take it."

"Me? What about you? I know I'm not the first. I know it. I think in her heart Alice might know it, too," Natalie screeched.

"I don't think so. I'm very, very good to Alice. I take care of her, because she needs to be taken care of. She would never believe anything bad about me. She might believe something bad about you, though. It's hard to say."

Natalie started to cry.

"Oh, God. Enough already. How much money do you want?"

"Ten thousand dollars. The security deposit for that shitty apartment wiped out all of my reserves."

"Ha ha. How about a thousand? That should give you a little extra for groceries this month."

"That's not enough. You know it isn't enough. I can't find a job." Natalie wiped her eyes with her hand smearing her mascara. "I've looked everywhere. I can't find anything."

"Beg me," John said.

"What?"

"Beg me. Get on your knees and beg. Make me believe you need the money."

Natalie stared at him. Slowly, she began to lower herself to the floor. "Please. Please. I need more money. I can't live like this. I need some help. Please."

"I've always liked the view of the top of your head. A woman doing what a woman should do," John took two fingers and tipped Natalie's face up. "You look horrible. You really should get it together. I'm feeling generous. I'll give you three thousand. Not a penny more. You weren't that good. Now say, 'Thank you, John' and go away like a good little girl."

"Thank you, John. When will you give me the money?"

"I'll let you know. Probably in a few weeks. I want you to think about what you've done. You need to consider a life change. We'll meet at that little coffee shop on the corner."

"Three weeks is too long. I have bills."

John sighed, "I'm not going to go out of my way for you." He opened his wallet. "Here's a thousand. You're just going to have to make it last until I can get to the bank."

She grabbed the money out of his hand. "You're a bastard."

"Now, now. Don't make me rethink giving you more money. Oh. And I'm pretty sure you've been making prank calls to my home phone. How about you stop doing that? It's upsetting to Alice."

Natalie slammed the door on her way out.

The conversation had been the second-worst one she had ever had in her life.

The worst conversation being when she had confessed the affair to her husband. Right after the first begging conversation with John.

The children had been upstairs in their room. She wanted them to be home, because she thought he would listen to her calmly. To protect the children.

She was mistaken.

*   *   *

Six Months Previously

She had set the pan on the stove to warm. She was planning on cooking ground beef for a quick, simple dinner.

She looked at her husband and began, "I have something to tell you. I need you to be calm, but it's important that you know."

He responded, "If you are about to tell me that you are a lying, cheating whore. I already know that." His face grew red. "I need you to get the fuck out of my house. Get the fuck out of my life. I'm not staying with you. I don't trust you. You've ruined our entire family!" He threw a glass at the wall. As it shattered, he said, "And for what?!? That piece of shit, John Smith! We used to talk about what a shitbag he was. What did I do to deserve this? What did I ever do to you?!?"

She whispered, "Nothing. Nothing. I just needed some attention. I just needed someone to see me."

"Get the fuck out. You needed some attention. I never want to see you again. Don't expect anything from me. Get out of my house."

"I'm not leaving until we work this out," she said semi-firmly.

"The fuck you aren't." He walked into the master bedroom and threw open the window. He began to toss her clothes onto the front lawn. Her things. She ran outside to collect them. He locked the door behind her.

She heard her children crying behind her. "Daddy, what's going on? Why are you and mommy fighting?"

Her husband answered, "Your mother is an evil person. I'm so sorry. I'll take care of you."

She put the things her husband had thrown out into the car. It wasn't everything. She looked at the mishmash of her belongings in the backseat and laid her head on the steering wheel and began to cry. Huge, never-ending sobs. She looked up and thought she could see her children's faces staring out at her through the living room picture window.

Still sobbing, every breath feeling like her gut hit her heart, she put the key into the ignition and started the car. She began to drive with tears blurring her vision. She turned onto the highway and began driving to nowhere.

She drove for about an hour until her mind cleared and she saw an exit sign with hotels listed. She picked a Holiday Inn Express to park at. Nothing super fancy.

"Hi. I'd like a room for the night," Natalie said.

"Great. I just need a form of ID and a card to put the room on," the desk clerk responded.

"Perfect." Natalie put her driver's license and debit card on the hotel shelf before her.

The clerk started punching in keys and then swiped her card. "Ma'am, I'm sorry, but your card has been declined."

"What?"

"Your card has been declined."

"No. No. Noooo... Plenty of money in that account. Ummmm... try this one," Natalie said as she pulled out the joint MasterCard she and her husband used.

"Ma'am...I'm sorry. This card has been declined. How would you like to pay for this room?" the clerk stated.

"I don't have another card and I don't have money."

"I apologize because we don't have anywhere for you to stay."

"Can I sleep in my car in your parking lot?"

The clerk stared at her. "No, Ma'am. We will call the police. I need you to leave. Have a great day."

"How am I supposed to have a great day?!? I need a room. I have nowhere to stay," Natalie whispered.

"You also have no money," the clerk responded.

"You don't know me. You don't know anything about me," Natalie started to cry.

"I know you have no money. You need to leave or I will call security."

"I'm going. I'm going," Natalie replied.

She went to her car and drove for a few more minutes. She found a park with no one around. She pulled a heavy sweater out of the back seat and folded it together to make a pillow and laid down upon it.

She didn't know where she would be tomorrow. She didn't know what she would eat tomorrow. She knew she would survive. She would see John and explain the situation. He would make everything right. He would take care of her.

Since the day she left, she hadn't seen her children. That was an ache and a burden she carried with her.

Chapter Twenty-two

Detective Morrison

orrison sat at his cluttered desk finishing up the police report from the Smith vandalism. His next step would be to contact Ms. McInroe and let her know that although charges wouldn't be pressed, she needed to figure out a better way to express her anger.

"Why are you sticking your neck out for this broad?" his commander asked. "She likely won't get jail time. It's not a big deal. If the wrong people find out you're blackmailing vics into not making charges, you're going to be in a world of hurt."

"Why do you care? No one will find out. Everything is solved and no harm done."

"Morrison, I've been married four times. I completely understand doing stupid shit for a woman. I just don't understand why this broad is worth it. Why is this the one that you would risk your career for?"

"She feels bad about what she did. She wears it on her face," Morrison said.

"You must be a poet now."

"Aw...man. Get outta here. Let me finish my report and make some calls."

Morrison thought back to his divorce. Although it had been three years ago, the situation still pained him. When he and his wife first separated, he remembered the constant feelings of inadequacy interspersed with anger. The picking up of the phone and starting to dial the numbers and hanging up because he didn't know how to apologize. Every word on his tongue felt foreign and useless.

His now ex-wife refused to speak to him about anything except for details on child-rearing or the splitting of their almost non-existent assets. His daughter screamed at him or sobbed that he didn't love her anymore. His son's simple questions that Morrison couldn't answer, "What's happening? Why don't you live with us anymore? Don't you still love us?"

He called his kids yesterday. His daughter refused to even speak to him on the phone. According to the court order, he could have forced it. But, he didn't know what to say to her anyway. His son liked his mom's new boyfriend, which was a different type of stab to the heart.

All for a cheap fling. One. One time that meant nothing and ruined his world.

Morrison felt sure that guys like Smith had girls on the side throughout their lives and never got caught. Or, if they did, their wives would never leave them and turn a blind eye. Life was different for rich people. Rich people took what they wanted. If they got caught, they just flung money at the problem until it went away.

He felt a certain kinship with Ms. McInroe. They had both destroyed their lives without truly understanding what their actions would mean. There were no mulligans for ordinary people. Average people lived their lives with all of their mistakes.

Morrison dialed the phone. "Ms. McInroe? This is Detective Morrison. I have news about your case."

"Please, tell me it's good news."

"It is. He won't press charges. He doesn't want to explain to his wife why you would trash his car."

"Alice wouldn't understand anyway. She thinks the sun rises and sets on John. I guess I did, too, for a while. He's one of those slick-tongued guys, you know?"

Morrison ignored the double entendre. "I would advise that you stay within the bounds of the law. He also can press charges any time within the next year, but I doubt that he will. I think the matter is settled in his mind."

"Thank you so much. I would offer to pay for the damage, but I don't feel bad," Ms. McInroe stated, sounding mildly feisty.

Morrison laughed, "I understand. If you ever feel like using a baseball bat on anything again, give me a call first."

"Are you asking me on a date? A vandalism date? I think that's a little unethical."

"Uh…no. I'm not. Sorry. I was just…" Morrison stammered.

"Flirting. You were just flirting a little," Ms. McInroe responded. "It's ok. I like being treated normally. It's a nice change. I don't know if you've ever been through a divorce."

"I have."

"It's so hard. The worst part is that people choose sides. Friends you have had your whole life choose sides. And if you are the bad person?" Morrison cringed when she said that word, "No one chooses your side. I think it's worse if you're a woman."

"I don't know about that."

"It is," she insisted. "People forgive men, because men are expected to mess up. Women can't be forgiven. Even now, we wear the scarlet letter. Did you ever read that book?"

"I'm not that into reading," Morrison answered truthfully.

"Oh. I just wonder how far we've come from those times. Women still get publicly shamed," she stopped. "I'm sorry. I'm ranting. I've taken up enough of your time. Thank you for getting back to me. I appreciate this more than you can know."

"It's not a problem. Have a great day." Morrison hung up the phone feeling like he had helped someone out today instead of just shuffling papers around.

It was a nice feeling.

Chapter Twenty-three

Natalie

Driving home, she answered her ringing phone. Detective Morrison said, "Hey, I know we just hung up, but I wanted you to know that I was definitely flirting. And, I would like to have dinner with you. I want to be clear about that."

"I don't even know your first name."

Morrison laughed, "It's Sam. Sam Morrison."

"I'm not ready to date anyone, yet."

"It's just dinner. As friends. Nothing more. Cross my heart. Hope to die. I completely understand how it feels to go through a divorce. Although, I gotta say, I'm not a huge fan of your taste in men."

"Oh, God. I don't ever want to think about John again. You don't know how hateful he's been," she said.

"He strikes me that way. Also, are you driving? You can't talk on the phone while you're driving. It's against the law. I don't want to have to write another report about you."

"Bluetooth, baby. One of the few things I still have after getting kicked out of my house."

"I just wanted to make sure," Sam Morrison said.

"Okay. Let's go to dinner. Don't make me regret this," Natalie warned.

"I wouldn't think of it. How about tonight? Eight? I know this great little Italian restaurant," Sam Morrison said.

"I see that you aren't wasting any time."

"I don't want you to change your mind."

"Do I strike you as a fickle woman?"

"You strike me as a beautiful, smart woman who has made some mistakes."

"Text me the address. I'll be there. As friends," she said.

"As friends."

*   *   *

She arrived at the restaurant a few minutes early. She tugged at the bottom hem of her dress. She shouldn't have changed. He would start to think that this was a date, but it felt *nice* to care about her appearance. To do her hair. Putting on make-up had always been a ceremony she enjoyed. She looked around and saw Detective Morrison at the corner table.

Sam, she amended.

He stood up from the table and waved to her. Then, he quickly thrust his hands into his pants pockets before pulling them out again and running them through his hair.

"I thought I would be the first one here," Natalie said.

"Not in your life. I'm always early. I was nervous that you might not show up, so I wanted to make sure I was here when you got here. I've been waiting for about thirty minutes," Sam said.

"That long?"

"I was nervous. It's been a long time since I've been to dinner with a female friend. I didn't know what to wear. I had to call my thirteen-year-old niece for advice."

"You don't have a daughter to call?"

"I do, but it's complicated. She completely blames me for the divorce. Probably, rightfully." Morrison pulled the chair opposite his out for Natalie. He sighed, "She still isn't talking to me. I don't want to force it."

Natalie slid into the booth. "I completely understand. I haven't seen my kids in a while and it's literally breaking my heart. When I do talk to them on the phone, I don't even know what to say."

"Do you want to talk about it? About what happened?" Sam asked.

"That's a very chick question."

"I'm a police detective. It's in my nature to ask. You don't have to talk about it if you don't want to. I'm just having a hard time understanding how someone like you could ever be attracted to that asshole, Smith. I need you to make *me* understand because maybe that's why I can't find a significant other," he paused. "I guess it could also be the child support, alimony, and the fact I work about sixty hours a week. I'm a total catch."

"You've been very kind to me. That's always attractive in a man. As for John… I don't know. I lost my mind. The kids were getting older. I felt like my husband didn't see me anymore. I felt like he just looked at me like his kids' mom. He hadn't even touched me in forever. No sex in months. When we first got married, we used to go to bed naked. Now, we both wear pajamas. Or, we did, when we slept in the same bed."

Natalie felt her face redden, "I'm sorry. That's embarrassing and too much information."

He waved her off. He said, "You're beautiful." Pausing for a moment, he continued, "I totally get it. I made a mistake, too, that ended my marriage. I guess that's why I wanted to reach out to you. I know how it feels to lose everything."

She said, "I was so stupid. John started to pay attention to me. He's my best friend's husband. Of all the people in the world, I chose him to cheat with." She shook her head, "He would pull me aside and compliment me or leave his hand on my arm a little too long. It's so ridiculous. It really is. I'm a cliche."

She continued, "It felt nice to be wanted. The first time he kissed me, I should have stopped it. So many times, I could have stopped it. I should have stopped it. In the end, he didn't even care about me. I think he just wanted to see if he could do it. The ultimate conquest, you know?"

"All affairs seem to start the same way and end the same way. And destroy families in the same way. My ex-wife caught me in bed with another woman. She came home early. Thankfully, the kids were staying at their grandma's house. I don't have an excuse. I was happy. I was just bored," Sam said.

"They say if you cheat once, you will cheat again."

"I don't know who 'they' are. It's not worth it. I don't even talk to the woman I had an affair with anymore. I can't look her in the eye. I can barely look myself in the eye."

"I hate John so much. I'm really not crazy. I promise. I don't normally trash other people's property. He broke me. I always thought I was strong, but I allowed him to break me," Natalie said. She looked down and found her fingers twisting through the paper napkin.

"Does his wife know?"

"Alice? Maybe. I don't know how she can't know. John always has someone on the side that he's seeing. He takes care of Alice, though. He really does. He's actually very sweet with her. He might care for her." She took a sip of her wine. "I miss her the most. Alice. She's a good person, but I can't look at her or talk to her," she stopped speaking for a moment. "Would it be okay if we talked about something else? I don't want to think about this anymore."

"What would you like to talk about?" Sam asked.

"You. How about you?" Natalie answered.

"Meh. I'm not very interesting. Let's talk about you instead. What kind of music do you like?"

"That is the lamest conversation change I've ever heard. Seriously, lame. Also, classical," Natalie answered.

Natalie and Sam talked throughout the night and ended up closing the restaurant down. After walking her to her car, Sam said, "I'd like to see you again 'as friends', if that's okay."

"I would like that. Send me a text next time you are off."

He saluted her. "Will do."

Chapter Twenty-four

Alice

"Alice, I'm so glad you could meet me for lunch. We must stay connected to each other. I want to make sure that everything is going right for you," Alice's father, Daniel, said.

"Hi, Daddy. It's always good to see you."

"You know I love having a monthly lunch with my girl. How are you feeling? How's John?"

"John is doing ok, I think."

"You think?"

"He's been working horrible overtime hours, so I don't see him much. He's a little stressed out and a little distracted, but that's to be expected."

"To be expected?"

"Because he just became first chair on an important trial. He's staying late all of the time with his assistant. I hardly see him anymore. When I do, he's a little short and a little snappy with me," Alice explained.

"A little short and snappy? What does that mean? I will talk to him if you need me to. He hasn't earned the right to be short and snappy with you," Daniel said.

"Daddy, sometimes you can't fix everything for me."

"I've yet to find a problem I can't fix for you."

"That's not your job. I can do things on my own."

"Sweetheart, it's not about whether it's my job. It's about whether John is taking care of you. He needs to be doing his job. The job he promised me that he would do when I allowed him to marry you."

"Has John said anything to you about what's going on?"

"No. But I can make him talk to me. I have my ways." Daniel raised his eyebrows at Alice.

Alice threw her head back and laughed. "Daddy, you are so silly. Please let me handle this on my own. I'm a big girl now. I know you don't want to believe that, but I am."

Daniel covered her hand with his. "You will always be my baby girl. I will always take care of you. Let me know what I need to make everything right for you and I will. I will talk to John about how he needs to treat you better."

"Please, don't do that," Alice pleaded.

"I will," Daniel commanded. "I know what's right for you and I'm going to do it."

"Daddy…"

"This is non-negotiable. I will fix this for you. It's what I do. I love you, sweetheart."

"I love you, too."

"Now tell me how things are going at work…"

Alice obliged, giving her father all the information John never wanted to hear.

Chapter Twenty-five

Jessica

essica watched her last boyfriend's house. She felt the snakes in her stomach start to slither as she sat in her car across the street. Adam didn't deserve this house. This family. He had made promises to her. To Jessica.

She watched until it was time.

Adam's wife left for work around eight a.m. She took the children with her. Probably to drop off at daycare. Jessica wasn't concerned about the wife's actual whereabouts. She just wanted the house empty. The Jacobs used a keyless entry system. The wife wasn't cautious with covering her hands when she input it. Jessica had seen the code several times. The wife was always too busy yelling at the children to worry about security.

She felt the bolt withdraw and unlock. The dog started barking. Earlier in the day, she had purchased some chuck roast at the market. She pulled it out of her purse and unwrapped it. As she entered the house, she threw it at the dog, who immediately pounced and began to snarfle it down.

The house was foreign to her in the sense that she had never been inside. Thankfully, before the Jacobs had purchased the house, their realtor had filmed a virtual walkthrough. After the house sold, the video remained available on a commercial website. Jessica watched it several times, memorizing the layout of the house.

Going directly to the kitchen, she opened the refrigerator door to look for Adam's insulin. He stored it in the left door tray. Fourteen vials neatly arranged. Each one marked with a felt pen for a date. It looked like a female's handwriting. The wife intruding once again. Always intruding.

Jessica picked up the vial dated for today and the next three just in case. In the backpack, she had a syringe and a few vials of U-500 insulin. Super insulin. Five times as concentrated as normal. If Adam used his usual amount, he would put himself into a diabetic emergency. Jessica hoped it would cause seizures. He deserved to suffer for the way he had cast Jessica aside. However, she would accept anything that ended in death. Even if that death came more quickly than he deserved. She didn't need to be picky.

Using the syringe, she withdrew the medication currently in the small refrigerator vials. She emptied the prescribed insulin into the sink. Next, she inserted the needle into the U-500 vial and drew out the super insulin. Carefully, she refilled Adam's vial with the new drug. After finishing, she examined her handiwork. She saw a small mark where she had punctured it, but didn't think anyone else would notice.

More importantly, Adam would die from low blood sugar. Not drugs. Not a gunshot. This was NOT her first rodeo. No one would be suspicious.

She spent fifteen minutes swapping the medication, but no one was due home for hours. She walked through the house opening doors and touching his things. Things he loved. He loved these *things*. *These things*. He loved them more than he had ever loved her.

She walked into his daughter's room. Three months old, if that. She, no… it. It didn't do much more than poop, eat, and sleep. He chose this life over her. She leaned over the crib and spat into it.

His bedroom was two doors down from the baby. The door to his bedroom stood open. The bed disheveled from last night's sleep. The wife couldn't be bothered to make the bed before she left for "work." She went to the closet and touched the clothes inside. On a hanger, she found a piece of lingerie. A pink nightie. She took off her clothes and slipped the silk onto her body. She ran her hands over her body encased in Adam's wife's nightie.

Turning around, she walked to the unmade bed. She threw the covers aside and laid on the dirty sheets thinking about the times she had spent with Adam. Remembering lunchtime hotel rooms chosen on the other side of town. She pulled her hands up her body and grasped her breasts. She held them for a minute, stroking her nipples. One hand slithered down her stomach. Into the ripeness between her legs.

When she climaxed, she envisioned Adam's death. She thought about John. John who needed her so much. John who also had a worthless wife.

Jessica gathered her clothes. She walked to her car, still wearing the nightie.

*   *   *

Adam left the house with the dog leashed. He stumbled as he went down the pathway from his house to the street. He shook his head as if to clear it and then glanced back at the house. He continued on.

The dog started to whine and pull back towards the house. "Come on, boy. You love your walk. It's good for both of us."

Lucky started barking and grabbed part of the leash and pulled it towards the house. "Lucky, stop it. We'll just go for a short walk, okay? Super short. I'm not feeling that well. I'm probably just tired, but I feel a little groggy." Lucky stared at Adam and proceeded to lick his hand. "I don't want Anne to walk you. She will just say she knew she would be the one taking care of you. You know I had to fight for you. So, just do your business super-fast and we will go right back home."

Lucky whined one more time, but acquiesced.

Jessica watched Adam continue with his daily walking routine. She followed him at a safe distance. Far enough away that he wouldn't see her, but she could still see him. He stumbled twice more, but never turned to go back to the house.

He wandered onto the multi-use path that wound through the park. The same one he used previously. Jessica watched him take the bottom of his shirt and wipe his face. His face turned a dark red. Sweat dribbled down the back of his neck, wetting his T-shirt. She didn't think it would take much longer.

He stumbled again. Tripping over his own feet. He righted himself, walking like a drunkard along the path. A few minutes later, he fell to the ground, dropping the dog's leash. "Lucky, wading do maman. Wading do maman!" Lucky pushed his snout to his owner's face and whined. "Wading do maman," Adam repeated without any real emphasis.

Adam's muscles began to seize. His hands turning into claws. His arms slamming the dirt around him. Spittle starting to ooze out his mouth. Lucky began to bark, trying to signal for help.

Jessica stepped forward and towered over his twitching body. "You deserve this. You are a fucking coward. Your life would have been better with me. I would have taken care of you." She smelled deeply through her nose. "Looks like you crapped yourself."

She waited until he stopped moving. The dog laid down by his master's side with his head on Adam's stomach and began to keen. Jessica bent down and unleashed the dog. "Go on, move."

Lucky wouldn't move. He just raised his head towards the sky and howled. Jessica kicked him in the ribs. "Get out of here!" she screamed.

Lucky ran.

Adam had the disservice to fall in the middle of the path. Jessica grabbed his feet and began to pull him towards the side of it. When she had dragged him a few feet away, she covered him with an assortment of branches and leaves. She hoped no one would find him until morning. He needed to be out here on his own for a while. She hadn't felt a pulse, but it was always better to make sure a person was given enough time to die.

Chapter Twenty-six

Detective Morrison

"Where exactly was the body found?" Morrison looked around at the crime scene.

A CSI tech motioned him over. "Just off the dog trail. The wife called 911 when he didn't come home from walking the dog last night. No one looked for him last night because..."

"Because we don't search for adults until they have been missing for more than eight hours and his wife may have been happy to have a few hours to herself." Morrison looked around. "Where's the dog?" he asked.

"Don't know. Looks like it might have run off. It was a rescue that had only been with the family a few months."

Morrison poked around a little more. "Who was the initial responding officer?"

"Me. Over here."

Looking over towards the voice, Morrison saw a younger officer standing off to the side. "Good to see you again. What happened?"

"Another dog walker found the body around 5:30 a.m. We are still waiting for the coroner to pinpoint the time of death and cause of death."

"Where's the M.E.?" Morrison asked. The officer pointed towards the medical examiner standing to one side and making notes on a tablet.

"What are your preliminary findings?"

"Signs of a seizure."

"Such as?"

"Vomit around the mouth. Bowels have been let go. It looks like he may have convulsed hard enough to snap a few bones," the medical examiner replied.

"Natural causes? If he was prone to seizures and had one while he was out by himself, it could result in death," Morrison mused.

The younger officer piped up. "I dunno. It seems convenient for the body to be so far off the path and covered up with random leaves and stuff. The body was probably lying here since last night and dozens of people passed it. I would think that if he died of natural causes, he would have been easier to find. It's just luck that he was found so quickly. He could have sat here for days."

Morrison rolled his eyes. "You could have started with that information instead of wasting my time."

"Sorry, I was just trying to be complete in my report."

"Whatever. Have we ID'd the body yet?"

"Yes, sir. Adam Jacobs. He had his wallet in his back pocket."

"I assume the family hasn't been notified?"

"Nope. We are still just interviewing potential witnesses. Everyone is more than happy to wait for the detective on the scene to make the notification."

"Understood. I will go ahead and do it."

Morrison called in and reported to his commander. "Other than the body being found a little off the trail, there aren't any other signs of homicide. I'll wait until the coroner gets back to me, but I think this could have just been natural causes. The guy just picked a bad time to go for a walk and his health got to him."

"Thanks for the update. Go ahead and make the notification. See what the family has to say," his commander responded.

Walking over to the address listed on the driver's license, Morrison knocked on the door of a two-story house. A bungalow with a dormer. Traditional Chicago-style. Same house replicated many times on the block.

He glanced at his watch. Seven a.m. Not a great way to start the morning. He rang the doorbell. The door opened almost immediately.

The lady answering the door started to vomit out words before the door was fully open. "Are you here about Adam? Have you found him? Is he ok? I've been waiting all night for information. He was acting a little funny when he set out for his walk. I was worried that maybe his sugar was off. He's diabetic."

"My name is Detective Morrison." He held up his badge.

"Have you found my husband? He walks the dog for an hour every night. He says it's therapeutic and good exercise, but last night he never came back. I've called his cell phone a hundred times, but he isn't picking up," the woman stated.

"I understand, ma'am. Can I come in for a moment?"

"Not until you tell me where my husband is."

"Ma'am, please."

Fear flashed through the woman's eyes. "Fine. Come in."

"What's your dog's name?" Morrison tried to calm her with easy questions.

"Lucky. What does it matter what my dog's name is? Where's my husband? Where's Adam?"

"I don't see the dog," Morrison commented.

"He took Lucky with him on the walk. I told you already. Are you even listening to me? Where is my husband? What does the damn dog have to do with anything?"

"When was the last time you saw your husband?"

"Last night around eight p.m., when he left to walk with Lucky. It was a little later than usual, but Adam enjoys walking at night. He feels safe with the dog to protect him. And he's always been one of those people that never believes anything bad will happen to him, you know?"

"I see. Ma'am, Mrs. Jacobs… I am truly sorry to inform you that we believe we have found your husband's body."

Mrs. Jacobs scoffed, "You believe? People believe in aliens. People believe in various gods that may or may not deserve their faith. I don't care what you believe."

"I apologize. I've been unclear. We have found your husband's body on a walking trail. We identified him through the driver's license we found in his wallet. That's why I'm here, ma'am. I will need you to do a positive ID when you feel up to it, but the driver's license picture matches the body."

She started laughing hysterically. High and off-pitch. Crazy laughter. "Stop saying the body. My god. You know, you don't know what the fuck you are talking about. Hold on one minute. I'm going to call Adam again on his cell phone. He'll pick up this time."

"Ma'am, nothing would please me more than for you to reach your husband right now. But, I am telling you..."

Mrs. Jacobs had her phone in one hand and made a halt sign with the other. Morrison could hear the ringing. It stopped and went to voicemail. She held up her forefinger in his face, "Just wait."

She redialed her husband's number. Morrison waited for her to leave a voicemail. "Adam! Adam, answer your phone right now! Right now! You're starting to scare me. The police are here," Mrs. Jacobs screeched.

"Ma'am, if we could sit down."

She slapped him across the face. "Don't tell me what to do. I'm tired of you. You can just go." She held her shoulders rigid as she left Morrison at the front door and moved towards the second floor.

Morrison made no outward reaction to the slap. He simply stated, "Ma'am, I need your help."

"For what?" She stopped halfway up the steep stairs.

"Does your husband have any enemies or people who might be angry with him?"

She took two steps down. "Yes. Yes. He has a restraining order against a young harlot. He made a mistake, but we're working on it. We're going to therapy. Do we have to go through this? I don't see how it helps. I'm trying to contact my husband."

"Yes, ma'am. I understand."

"That's all you can say to me? That's it! Fuck you! Fuck you!"

"Yes, ma'am. I understand."

"I HATE you. I will hate you forever. Forever. For these words that you have said to me," she continued to rage.

"Yes, ma'am. I understand."

"Do you? Do you?" she kept repeating the words. Over and over.

Morrison thought back to his divorce. To his ill-thought affair. To his studio apartment that he considered more of a cell than a living space. To the time lost with his children. To the love lost with his wife. To the love lost with his *living* wife. "I don't understand. Not really. I know that I am the monster in your closet. I know that you will hate me forever. I need *you* to understand that I am the person that can help you find out what happened. To help your family find closure. I don't have anything else that I can say. No other arguments."

She collapsed on the stairs. Her left hand took the brunt of the fall as she reached back to steady herself. "What. What exactly do you need. To know right now? Right now?" Her voice raw with emotion. "I don't know how I can help you right now. My children…"

Morrison crossed the threshold. He sat heavily on one knee. His knee communicated its anger about not following up with his doctor regarding arthritis that got worse every passing year. "Mrs. Jacobs, what's your first name?"

"Anne."

"Anne. May I call you Anne?"

She nodded her head once in affirmation.

"Anne. I am so sorry, but we believe there is a possibility that your husband has been murdered. We need your help to figure out the truth about what happened to him. Any information you can provide us with would be helpful. Anything. Please. Help us. I wouldn't be here, if I weren't sure."

Anne's eyes rolled up into her head and she fainted. Morrison caught her before she could complete her fall down the remaining steps.

*   *   *

"Jessica Allen," Mrs. Jacobs answered Morrison's question. Her voice hoarse, "Jessica Allen."

A patrol officer accompanied Mrs. Jacobs to the hospital. He called Morrison when she received clearance from the doctor to speak to the police. The sterilized room offered zero comforts to its current inhabitant. The white walls muting the intensity of any emotion expressed there. Morrison wished he could move this conversation to somewhere else. Anywhere else would be better. Instead, Morrison laid a calming hand on the sterile, white blanket. "Anne, who is that?"

"We had a restraining order against her. My h-h-husband had an affair with her. Skinny, pretty wench. He broke it off, when he found out I was pregnant with Carol. She kept calling and showing up at our house."

"Really?" Morrison raised an eyebrow.

"She would show up on our doorstop screaming crazy, ugly things."

"Like what?"

"That she and Adam were meant to be together forever. That Adam wouldn't know how to live without her. She said I could get in an accident with my children at any time. And where would Adam be then? I thought she was a former client who didn't get exactly what she wanted. I realized she and Adam had an affair, when she screamed vulgar things at me. He wouldn't admit to the affair until then. He just kept telling me to ignore her. That she would go away if we didn't pay her any attention."

"Vulgar things?"

"Don't make me say it," Anne responded tiredly. "I didn't believe her, until she described a birthmark that Adam has in his area."

"His area?"

"His pelvic area," Anne whispered.

"I see," Morrison responded. "How did she accept the restraining order?"

"Well. Or as well to be expected, I guess. I never saw her again," she paused. "Detective, can I see my husband? I need to be sure." She hesitated, "I just need to be sure, before I tell my children. I just need to be sure." She kept repeating the phrase as the floor nurse ushered Morrison out of the room.

Chapter Twenty-seven

Natalie

"What are you doing tonight?" Natalie picked up the phone to hear Sam Morrison's voice on the other end.

She smiled. "Aren't you supposed to start a phone conversation with pleasantries like hello?"

"Let's pretend that I did and we are on to the meat of the conversation. I ask once again. What are you doing tonight?"

"Nothing, I guess. I'm just at my apartment sitting on the couch. Preparing to watch the news."

"Don't watch the news. Only desperately bored people or old folks watch the news."

"Do you have a better idea?" Natalie asked.

She heard a sharp rap at the door to her apartment. She opened it and Sam was standing there with a bag of groceries.

"As a matter of fact, I do," he said as he made his way inside her apartment. "Point me to your kitchen."

"What are you doing here? My place is a mess. My kitchen is the size of a thimble."

"I am making you dinner and I brought you some extra groceries."

"Everyone seems to be feeding me lately."

"Mostly because you are way too skinny. Also, the appropriate response to a man arriving to make you dinner is thank you."

"Thank you," Natalie responded.

Sam started to forage through the cabinets. "You don't have much here. Where are your wine glasses?"

"Likely with my ex-husband."

"Ouch. Sorry about that. These will do just fine." Sam pulled out a couple of mismatched rocks glasses Natalie had recently picked up at a garage sale. He pulled a bottle of red wine out of the bag.

"I don't think I have a corkscrew."

"No matter. A boy scout is always prepared." Sam produced a wine key from deep within the bag and proceeded to pour them both a generous amount of wine.

"How can I help?" Natalie asked.

"Your job is to drink your wine and keep me company. I am about to make you my grandma's finest penne ala vodka. I emailed her for the recipe and she was more than happy to oblige."

Natalie laughed. Her apartment was small enough that she could curl into an afghan on the couch and still easily talk to Sam in the kitchen.

"What was your plan if I wasn't home?"

"I was going to leave the groceries on your doorstep with a note. Then call you and tell you to put them in the fridge."

"Someone might have taken them."

"I'm a police detective. I still have faith in the goodness of humanity. Most people won't steal groceries and if they do, it's because they need the food. If someone had taken them, I would have bought more for you. I would also have tried to track down who took them and buy more groceries for them."

"You're very kind."

"We need to take care of each other. That's what we're missing right now in life and politics. We've forgotten how to take care of each other. We've forgotten that the very core of being human means to be kind to others regardless of their circumstances or beliefs."

"A chef and a philosopher. Oh, and an excellent picker-outer of wine."

"I wouldn't want to be boring," Sam quipped. "Seriously, though, seeing the worst that humanity can do reinforces that most people are good people. Most people are horrified by the things I deal with every day."

"I'm surprised it doesn't make you cynical."

"It does to some people. A lot of people. But we deal with such a small portion of people in the world that it gives me hope. How many people ever need the services of the police because they are victims of a violent crime? Some people, of course. I want to help them out as much as possible. Because when I help them out, I help out those who have never been victims stay not being victims." Sam stopped and looked at Natalie, "I'm sorry. I'm probably boring you."

"Your commitment to your job and your commitment to people is amazing," Natalie said.

Sam scoffed.

"No, really, I mean it. I wish I believed in something as much as you do," Natalie said.

"Who's stopping you?" Sam asked.

"Uh...myself, I guess. I can't just randomly start believing in something. Especially, since I am far from perfect. Look what I did to my marriage, my family."

"Why do you think perfection has any part of belief?"

"I'd just feel like a hypocrite otherwise."

"No. Belief is a part of forgiveness, not perfection. Otherwise, I would be stuck at the bottom rung of life forever. This talk is too heavy for my pasta. My pasta will start to taste like sad. I know you said I didn't need your help, but why don't you put the salad together? We need to get onto sunnier topics like tomatoes," Sam said.

Natalie laughed and went to start cleaning and dicing the tomatoes. "Thank you for coming over. I really appreciate the company. I think the last time I had this nice of an evening was when we went out to dinner."

"You better watch out, because I could make this happen more often. I enjoy your company," Sam said sincerely.

"You're so silly," Natalie said. She kept smiling as she put the salad together.

Sam responded by swatting her on the butt with the spatula he was using.

"Hey! I said before we were only going to be friends!" Natalie squealed.

"That's why it was a friendly spatula swat and not a dirty one," Sam smirked.

"You are an absolute mess," Natalie said and threw a piece of cucumber at him that she had been slicing for the salad. He deftly grabbed it and ate it.

They finished putting dinner together soon after. Natalie set the table with the best of her garage sale finds, while Sam topped off the wine. They ate dinner and talked long into the night. Sam only left when he realized it was close to midnight.

Natalie sat on the couch with the last of her wine after Sam had left. She hugged herself. It was nice to spend time with a man and be seen for who she was. It had been a long time since she had felt valued.

Needed.

Maybe, wanted.

Chapter Twenty-eight

Alice

"I need you to tell me if I'm crazy."

"You're crazy," Ryan said.

"You are being super not helpful." Alice and Ryan sat at a small cafe situated around the corner from their office building. "I have some real concerns. Some real concerns that are probably silly. I am about eighty-five percent really worried about them."

"Soooo... less talk about your anxiety and more talk about what's causing it," Ryan said.

Alice kicked him under the table. "Thanks for being so understanding, jerk."

"For real. What's up?"

"John and I went to see Natalie yesterday."

"You and John?" Ryan asked incredulously. "One, why would you do that? Two, why would you bring John?"

"Uh...Because she's my friend and he's my husband."

"I understand the words coming out of your mouth. I'm just having a hard time comprehending them. Let's start with what happened?"

"That's what I don't understand. She screamed at me through the door. She wouldn't even let us in. She just kept cursing at me. Well…I thought she was cursing at me." Alice looked down. Her finger doodled in the condensation from her water glass. "I don't want to say what I'm thinking."

"Say it. Say it. For the love of everything holy. Say it," Ryan begged.

She looked up and looked at him hard. "Do you know what I'm going to say?"

"I have an inkling and I've been waiting for this for a very long time."

"I think…I think she wasn't talking to me at all. I think she was talking to John," Alice stammered. "I thought she was talking to me. Like she was answering my questions. But, I don't think she ever saw me or heard me."

"So, what's your conclusion?"

"I don't know why she would yell at John."

"Yes, you do."

"No, I don't," Alice said forcefully. "I really don't."

"You know, you just don't want to admit it. Alice, you know I'm still friends with Natalie. I know about everything that happened. I know who she cheated with. I think you do too."

"No."

"Yes."

"No."

"Yes. Why do you think Natalie is ignoring you? Why do you think she was talking to John and not you? Has John been telling you to check on your friend or telling you she's fine? Has he told you to ignore her?"

"I don't understand what you're saying. I don't believe you," Alice whispered.

"Yes. You really do."

"I don't. I just…John wouldn't do this to me."

"Wouldn't he? I think he would. I know he would. He isn't a great guy," Ryan stated.

"He's my husband. I took a vow. He took a vow. I don't think he would do that to me. Especially not with Natalie. She was my best friend. I don't know why she won't talk to me anymore. Nothing makes sense. None of it."

"Yes, it does. It makes sense. For a person who analyzes numbers and stats for her life's work, you sure can't analyze this very well. Everyone can see it. He's making a fool of you."

"I refuse to believe that. He's not making a fool of me. I'm sorry that I even brought it up. I need to trust my instincts. And, I need to trust my husband. He's just been working late a lot and I'm reading too much into it. I thought I liked being alone, but maybe I need a little more time with him."

"I understand that you feel a need to trust your husband. Alice, you need to think about yourself. Think *for* yourself."

"My instincts are clearly wrong. John would never do anything to hurt me."

Ryan sighed, "We almost had a breakthrough."

Alice said, "That new restaurant in town is making take-home duck dinners. Like whole ducks. I'll call John and tell him not to work late and we'll just have a nice dinner at home."

"Yeah, a nice dinner. That's what will fix all of your problems," Ryan murmured. "Alice, I want you to know that when you are ready to face what's happening, I'll be here for you."

Chapter Twenty-nine

Jessica

essie, I need you to pick up my car from the body shop over on 22nd. I just got a call that it's finally ready. They took their sweet time with it."

"Anything you want, John."

"You're a lifesaver."

"Do you want me to stop over at the liquor store and grab a bottle of wine on my way back?"

"That would be great."

Jessica opened her Uber app and requested a ride. It stated the vehicle would arrive in nine minutes. While she waited on the bench outside the building, the cold forced her to pull her scarf tight around her neck.

She called the number for Natalie McInroe that she had found in the court pleadings stored on the company's computer.

Natalie answered on the first ring, "Hello?"

"Hi, Natalie. I'm John's assistant, Ms. Allen. John asked me to call you. He wants to meet you in about thirty minutes over at the coffee shop by the park. He said you would know what that meant."

"25th and Lexington?"

"That's the one," Jessica said. "He wants to apologize for what happened and make everything right. He has a check for you. The amount that you two decided on."

"Finally. Thank God. Why isn't John calling me? Why are you doing it? Did he tell you what's going on?"

Jessica realized she should never have mentioned the money. She didn't need Natalie or John, for that matter, to know that she had eavesdropped on their last conversation. It would ruin Jessica's plans. "I don't know. You can talk to John about that. I'm sure he has an answer."

A long pause. "Ok. I'll meet him there."

*   *   *

Realizing it would be a few more minutes before the Uber driver picked her up, Jessica thought about the two years she spent wearing a uniform at that horrible boarding school. Two years pretending to be the good girl everyone wanted. Calling her mom at the scheduled time every week, whether or not her mother answered the phone didn't make a difference. Making Dean's List. Volunteering to feed the righteously poor at the church's food bank.

Her mom and Mark brought their new baby to Jessica's graduation in an RV. "We are now people of the world," her mom bragged. "We have been to almost twenty states. Our goal is to hit the entire continental United States. It's so great that Nicky gets to travel through the country and learn on the road!" Her mom pointed at the magnetic map on the side of the vehicle, boasting of all the states they had traveled.

"It's a little unconventional, but we love it. We sold the house last year. We still have all of your things, so don't worry! We put them into storage for you. It's so good to see you graduating and heading off to college. I'm so proud of you," Jessica listened to her mother ramble and inwardly rolled her eyes.

"Thanks, Mom. I know I've said it before, but it's important to me that you understand how sorry I am that I got caught doing those terrible things. I shouldn't have done it."

"You're sorry you got caught?" Mark asked.

"You know, because I shouldn't have done them in the first place?" Jessica answered.

Jessica's mom put her hand on her heart. "Oh, honey. I know that's what you meant. I'm so thankful that you're back on track." She reached up and tucked a piece of errant hair behind Jessica's ear. "Mark and I have been so worried about you. Your worth doesn't depend on some boy. You are enough. You are absolutely perfect just the way you are."

"Mom, stop being weird," she said without giving voice to her internal monologue of whether or not Mark cared about her personal well-being.

"I'm just so proud of the woman that you've become. I hope you know that you can always rely on yourself and you can always rely on us. We will always be here for you. I know you think you're grown now, but you'll always be my little girl. I just love you so much. I know I said some horrible things before. I was terrified for you at that point. This time apart has given me some perspective on how much I miss not having you around all the time."

"Mom, seriously, I need to get in line for graduation."

"I know, baby, I know. I just need to remember this moment."

Jessica graduated a respectable fifty-seven in her class of 122. She wasn't recognized for any awards at graduation. Nor was she disparaged.

After the ceremony, she found her parents and their new child standing on the side of the gym, looking useless. Her mom raised the camera again. "Smile!" she commanded before snapping another twenty pictures.

"Can we go? I'm ready to leave this place," Jessica said.

"Of course! We made a reservation at Fizzano's Italian Restaurant. We looked at the reviews and it sounds great. I know how much you love Italian."

"Sounds great, Mom. After that, can we just crash? I'm super tired."

"Absolutely. I think you're going to love the RV spot in the park we reserved for the next few nights. It's deep in the woods and so peaceful. We are just really connecting to nature right now."

Mark nodded dutifully.

*   *   *

They parked on the far side of Cuyaga Valley National Park in Ohio. "We can boondock," Mark explained. Then described the term as relying only on their RV with no sewer, water or electric hookups. No other travelers within their vicinity. "This RV put us back about eighty thousand. Worth every penny. Look over here. This is the generator. It runs everything in the RV..." Mark blathered on about how to hook everything up and disconnect it.

"Sweetheart, here's a tent for you to sleep outside. The RV just isn't that big. What with Nicky taking up most of the back area for a nursery. I hope you understand. You can sleep in the 'living room' if you prefer," Jessica's mom used apostrophe fingers for emphasis. "But, I just think sleeping under the nighttime sky will be so much more rejuvenating. You can decide your next steps in life while communing with nature."

Jessica rolled her eyes. "Will I at least be able to use the bathroom in the middle of the night, or will I have to pee in the poison ivy?"

"Don't be silly. We won't lock you out."

Jessica set up her tent and bid her parents goodnight. As she was closing the door behind her, she heard her mom ask Mark quietly, "You still have the gun by your bedside, right?"

Why would Mark need a gun at the ready? For protection? Or, did they plan to kill her out here in the middle of nowhere? Mark would likely be just as happy to leave her corpse somewhere out here for the bears to find. Jessica knew that he had never liked her. She could tell he was thrilled that he and her mom had started a new family without her.

She lay in her tent and watched the lights go off in the RV. The weather was abnormally hot for June. Her mom and Mark left the generator on to power the air conditioning. Never mind that Jessica was out in the woods sweating her ass off.

Boarding school forced her to learn patience. Learn that timing mattered as much as intent. In the last two years, anyone who crossed her ended up losing things or accidentally hurting themselves. At least two girls left the school with their minds bordering on a psychotic break.

Tonight, she would be patient. She would be perfect. She would not be punished.

When the moon was high in the sky, she entered the RV. If anyone awoke, she would claim she needed to use the bathroom. She listened to the wild snores of Mark and the quieter sleep snuffles of her mother. She walked through the tiny hallway. She passed the wall that signaled the differentiation between the living room and the sleeping area. She stared down at the people who had sent her away. She watched them sleep.

She backed into the small living area. The smoke detector/carbon monoxide detector flashed red at regular intervals. Climbing onto a chair, she took out the battery and repositioned the detector on the ceiling. On her way out, she lifted the sleeping baby from his bed and deposited him in the tent.

Over the last year as conversations with her mother had turned to the RV and Nicky, Jessica realized she would never be necessary for this new family. Her mother and Mark planned to leave her behind. Probably, they would go so far as to pretend she didn't exist. That's when she started researching RV deaths. Carbon monoxide continued to be a number one source of concern for the average RV user.

She went to the generator outside and looked at the plastic tubing Mark had left near it. He had visions of creating a mobile rain harvesting unit which he had regaled her with details all afternoon. She picked up the hose and attached it to the generator. She pushed the long tube into the open window and duct-taped it in place.

The generator continued to run. Filling the RV with carbon monoxide.

She went back to her tent. Sitting cross-legged at the entrance with the child at her back. When morning came, she called 911. "Hello? Hello? I need someone to help me!"

"911. What's your emergency?"

"Something happened to my mom and my stepdad. They aren't moving. I don't know what to do. We're in an RV out in the woods. I volunteered to sleep in an outside tent, because there wasn't enough room. I went to go check on breakfast and I found them."

Jessica purposefully hitched her voice, "My little brother is sick too, but he's still moving. Please hurry. I don't know how to help them. What if they don't wake up?" Jessica wailed. She wanted to make sure to put on the best performance of her life.

"What campsite are you at exactly?" the operator asked.

"G? I think campsite G?" Jessica answered.

"Is anyone responsive at all? How long ago did you find them? Do they have a pulse? Please answer my questions, so I can send help as soon as possible," the operator continued to ask more questions.

"What? What? I can't hear you," Jessica pretended to hear interference on the phone. She hung up, tired of answering inconsequential questions.

As she sat there, she remembered the hose still connecting the generator to the RV. She ran to disconnect it. She hid the hose in one of the outside storage compartments that contained other random non-essential tools.

Jessica waited for the ambulance and considered her future. Hopefully, she was still in her mom's will. Supposedly, a life insurance policy existed. A romantic wedding gift from Mark. If all the money had gone to the child behind her, she would have mistimed the situation. She planned to drop the baby off with Mark's parents. She wasn't going to be saddled with her mom's mistakes for the rest of her life. But, she didn't want to punish the baby just for being born.

Later, when the bodies had been released to the funeral home and the baby had been installed elsewhere, she looked up the police report. It had been marked as an accidental death. They found the carbon monoxide detector without batteries and assumed Mark had failed in his husbandly duties to ensure a safe environment for his family. A note even appeared on the report that people should always make sure their detectors were working. She figured someone would pull all these "accidental deaths" together and put out a public service campaign.

Well, good for them. Carbon monoxide poisoning was a serious issue.

It could kill almost an entire family.

*　　*　　*

After being dropped off at the body shop by the Uber driver, Jessica picked up John's car and headed towards the coffee shop. She wanted to be on time for her rendezvous with Natalie McInroe.

Chapter Thirty

Natalie

Natalie paced the length of her apartment back and forth. Ten steps one way. Then, ten steps the other. She was waiting for the appointed time to go to the coffee shop and see John. This would be the last time she saw him. She just needed a little extra money to get up off her feet.

She picked up her phone to call Ryan and set it down again. She shook her head. Calling Ryan wasn't a good idea.

Ten more steps this way.

Natalie picked up the phone and held it to her heart.

Ten more steps that way.

She wanted to talk to Ryan. She needed to talk to someone.

Ten more steps this way.

She pulled up Ryan's contact number on her phone and hit call.

"Hey, girl! What are you doing, princess?" Ryan answered on the first ring.

"I'm going to see John and get more money from him," Natalie stated matter-of-factly.

"No. No. No. You're not. We talked about this. I will help you out. Do not ask him for anything more. He isn't worth your time. Please, tell me you aren't asking for money just so you can see him," Ryan responded.

"I'm not. He owes me this money. He owes me. He can't treat me like this. He can't treat women like this and have there be no consequences. This is the last time. I promise. I just want him to know that he can't get away with this," Natalie explained.

"I think that you might be getting addicted to free money. That's what addicts say. Just one more. Girl. You're better than that. You are. Don't go. Don't do it."

"You aren't going to talk me out of this."

"Why did you call me then?"

"I think I need to come clean to Alice. I've tried several times, but I can't do it on my own. Would you be willing to help me? I need support and Alice will need support, too."

"You are putting me in a super awkward position."

"That doesn't sound like a no."

Ryan sighed, "It's not a no. Can we just make sure there's alcohol involved?"

Natalie smiled, "I wouldn't have it any other way."

"Just tell me a time and place and I'll be there."

"Thank you so much. I appreciate you so much. You have no idea," Natalie said.

"Whatevs. Love you, girl. You call Alice and let me know the info."

"Will do. Thanks again. I owe you!"

"Yeah, you really do," Ryan said as he hung up the phone.

Ten steps this way. Ten more that way.

Natalie pulled Alice's name up in her contacts and hit the green button. The phone rang through to voicemail. "Hi, Alice. I have some things I need to talk to you about. Ryan is coming with me to give me some support. I tried to tell you before, but I wasn't strong enough. Please, forgive me. Please, forgive me for everything. I would tell you now, but I need to be strong and say it to your face. Can you meet me on Friday at Finnegan's? At seven? Let me know."

Ten steps this way. Ten steps that way.

Looking down at her watch, Natalie took a deep breath. It was almost time to meet John. She went into the bathroom and ran a brush through her hair and re-applied her make-up. She wanted John to realize what he threw away. She headed towards the door, grabbing her purse along the way. She would be at the coffee shop within fifteen minutes. She hoped John would be on time.

Chapter Thirty-one

Jessica

essica sat in the coffee shop, three booths over from Natalie McInroe. She watched Natalie pick up her phone several times and make calls. No one seemed to answer because she would put the phone down after a few seconds. Natalie waited a solid forty-five minutes for John to show up. Jessica thought that was a reasonable period of time to wait for John. An amount that showed respect for the man.

Natalie stood up and moved towards the exit.

Jessica followed.

Natalie began walking down the street towards an unknown location. Maybe to the bus station? Natalie didn't live in the neighborhood anymore and there didn't seem anywhere else for her to go.

Jessica quickened her pace to better follow her prey. She called out, "Hey, it's Natalie, right? Do you remember me? I work in John Smith's office?" Jessica pitched her voice to end in a question every time. Trying to indicate that she had no idea about this harlot's identity.

"Uh… yes. I'm sorry. You are?"

"Jessica! John's assistant? We spoke on the phone earlier. I think you came into the office once? Don't you remember me?"

"Oh, yeah, I'm just a little distracted right now. Wait. Wait. You set up the meeting with John. Why didn't he show up? I waited for almost an hour. It's really important that I see him."

"He didn't show? That's not like him. I hope everything is all right." Crossing her fingers that Natalie wouldn't call her bluff, Jessica pulled her cell phone out of her purse. "Give me one second. I'm going to call him right now and we can sort this whole thing out."

"No. No. I just… I just want to go home. I need to hurry to catch the next bus across town before it leaves," Natalie said. Jessica heard the tremor in Natalie's voice.

"Oh… hey… I know you're a client or something," Jessica said vaguely. "I can give you a ride, if you like. It's really no trouble."

Natalie pulled out her wallet and counted the bills inside. "I don't know. I don't want to be a bother."

"It's no bother! John would be mad at me, if I didn't help you out. He's such a great guy."

"Yeah, I'm sure. Look, I can't pay you. I'm down to my last little bit. I barely have enough for rent this month. I thought I was about to receive some extra cash, but I guess, once again, I depended on the wrong person."

"All the more reason you should let me help you." Jessica smiled, "There's no catch. I'm parked right around the corner. Come on, let me help you out."

"I…ok." Looking bereft, Natalie rattled off her address and followed Jessica to her car.

They rode in silence for several minutes. "Isn't this John's car?" Natalie asked.

"Oh, yeah. I had to pick it up, because someone threw paint on it and smashed it up a couple of weeks ago. It took forever to get fixed. Isn't that horrible?" Jessica answered.

"You picked up his car?"

"Who else would do it? I don't know if you have ever met his wife, but she just messes everything up. He compensates for her all the time. It's a little ridiculous."

More silence. Natalie waited until Jessica had stopped at the corner and got out of the car.

Natalie stepped out onto the curb. "Does Alice know?"

"Does Alice know what?"

"Does Alice know that you're having an affair with her husband?"

"What makes you say that?"

"I know how John thinks. I know his history. I know what it means when you're running random errands for him. Alice is a good person. I just want her to be treated better."

"Better than what?" Jessica asked.

"Better than how I treated her," Natalie looked at the ground, examining her shoes. She continued, "Don't be me. Don't beg for crumbs. For his leftovers. Be smarter. He isn't worth it. He's not."

Jessica looked around and saw no one on the street. She backed the car up at an angle. She pressed the gas pedal.

The car easily went over the curb and pinned Natalie between it and the corner stop sign where Jessica had dropped her off.

Natalie started to scream, "What are you doing?!?"

Jessica backed the car up. Natalie moved to run down the sidewalk, stumbling and favoring her right leg. Natalie continued to scream, "Stop it! What are you doing? Why are you doing this?"

Jessica aimed the hood of the car at Natalie as best as possible. She hit the gas and slammed into Natalie again. Natalie fell to the ground with the side of her head hitting the pavement with a satisfying thwack.

Pushing the car forward once more and back again, Jessica heard the soft watermelon splat of Natalie's head. She could feel the victorious thump under the vehicle. She felt Natalie's silence.

Natalie wouldn't cause John any more problems.

*   *   *

"Here's your keys. Your body shop does crappy work, though. The bumper fell off when I took it through the car wash," Jessica said.

"What? How the hell would a bumper just fall off?"

Jessica knew it fell off when a person pulled on it hard to make sure said person got rid of any possible evidence of running down another person. But she said, "Beats me. I don't know anything about cars."

"Goddamit. Give me one second and I'll call them back. They can fix their shitty work."

Alarmed, Jessica said, "You've got a lot on your plate. How about you let me take care of it for you?"

"My insurance paid good money and they can't even fix the fucking car. I'll just let them know exactly what I think of their services. Someone has to teach them about good work."

"That's exactly why you should let me take care of this. You're too angry. They will never fix it right if you yell at them."

"Ugh. Fine. But, if they give you any shit, just go to a different shop and we'll sue those fuckers."

"Understood." Jessica mentally tallied how much money she would need to take out of petty cash to fix the car. Likely no one would even notice. Everyone borrowed money from it for random non-business-related reasons. Besides, she had plenty of time to replace it before the monthly accounting.

Chapter Thirty-two

Detective Morrison

 know you are still working on the Adam Jacobs case. Have we conclusively decided that was a murder, by the way?" his commander asked.

"We haven't made any findings one way or the other. The whole thing feels off. I don't have enough evidence to prove a homicide," Morrison admitted. "The coroner keeps saying natural causes. Dude's blood sugar was off. Wife keeps saying no way he would have overdosed on insulin. I'm not sure what to think. I'm not sure there's enough evidence to go forward."

"So, write something for the file and push it forward to me. Stop looking for ghosts that don't exist. Sometimes people die."

"Again, it just doesn't feel right. I'm not ready to move on. The coroner says Adam Jacobs went into diabetic seizures because he had too much sugar in his blood. At my insistence, he's ruling it inconclusive as to whether it's a homicide or not."

"Stop. Why are you trying to make more work for yourself? Put the death down as natural causes and move on to the next mess."

"The dude was pretty healthy besides the diabetes. The wife says he was very careful with his insulin and that the correct number of vials are in the fridge. She says he wouldn't have done anything to put his health at risk. I also don't like that he was probably pushed off the side of the trail," Morrison mused.

"Is it possible that he just fell that way?"

"Possible, but not likely. There were branches and leaves covering him."

"He was having seizures. Is it possible that he accidentally rolled off the path? Who knows, maybe he saw something in the woods and decided to go check it out. Do you have any solid evidence that the body was physically moved?"

"There isn't any evidence that I can find that the body was pushed or pulled off. No track marks of any sort. The wind could have blown some stuff on him," Morrison admitted. "Other walkers could have erased the tracks."

"Not likely," the commander said.

"No, not likely," Morrison agreed, staring off into space.

"Good. Move on. File a report. Focus your attention on this new body."

"How is it that I'm the one who keeps catching these fucking cases? Doesn't anyone else in this department work?" Morrison groused.

"You seem to have some sort of connection with the vic. You filed a report that accused her for vandalism a month ago. But, you never went forward with filing. An uncooperative witness or something like that," his commander explained.

"What connection? What are you talking about? Who's the vic?" Morrison asked.

"Young lady by the name of Natalie McInroe."

"Are you shitting me? Natalie McInroe?"

"There is no shit to be had here, my friend. I figured since you had a connection with her that you would be the most logical detective to move forward."

"Do we have any idea about what happened?" Morrison asked.

"Hit and run," his commander answered.

"Give me the address. I'll go check out the scene," Morrison said. "I'll do this. I will do this." Morrison kicked the desk his commander was sitting at.

"What do you think you're doing?"

"I knew her. I just knew her. She was my...friend."

"I'll assign another detective. I don't want you near this thing, if you're going to be emotional."

*   *   *

Morrison always felt that when someone died, there should be more than the usual amount of life. Something more should happen. Something that marked the end of life, so everyone understood how this death impacted the world.

Police roped off the scene where Natalie died with crime tape. Natalie's body lay underneath a tarp in a grotesque imitation of decency. A few officers milled around, but hit and runs never brought out significant police activity. The chances of discovering the perpetrator slim.

"Witnesses?" Morrison barked at the nearest officer.

"None that we have found. We are still trying to talk to everyone. It happened in the middle of the day in a working-class neighborhood. Everyone was at work or minding their own business," the officer said.

"Cameras? Any kind of camera in the vicinity?"

"Did you miss the part about this being a working-class neighborhood? People don't have thousands of dollars worth of security cameras here. The city doesn't invest in this part of town either."

"I can't believe that we have nothing. No one saw anything? There must be three hundred people living in this area," Morrison stated.

"Kitty Genovese effect. You know how people are. No one wants to get involved," the officer responded.

Morrison nodded reluctantly.

"Do we have anything? Anything at all? Give me something," Morrison pleaded. "She can't die this way."

"We found a little black paint flecked off on her clothes. Looks like the perp jumped the curb with the car and pinned her between the sign and the vehicle. Then, backed up and ran her over to make sure she was done." The officer paused, "We are taking pictures of the tire marks on the curb and sending them to the lab. Hopefully, it will come back to a match that we can track down."

"Wait. Did you say black paint?"

"Yes, sir."

Morrison saw a glimmer of being able to make an arrest. He was sorry he couldn't help Natalie more. He would try. He would try with everything he had. Likely, he would fail one more woman in his life. He may not be good at life, but he was terrific at failure.

Smith's car was black. And, it had been vandalized by Natalie.

Chapter Thirty-three

Alice

"Oh, Alice. I can't believe it. I honestly can't believe this happened," Ryan pulled Alice into a bear hug.

"What are you talking about?" Alice asked. She had just gotten into work that morning. She arrived one minute early. People only walked into work early thirty-two percent of the time.

"Don't you know? You haven't heard. Ohmigod. You haven't heard," Ryan ran the sentences together so quickly. It could have just been one word.

"Ryan, I need you to calm down. You're scaring me," Alice spoke quietly, yet firmly. She learned this technique through several years of conversations with her therapist. She needed to speak in a way that conveyed her sense of urgency and communicate that the intended target, Ryan, would tell her the necessary information. Her therapist insisted this was key to managing her anxiety. Helping her to express her feelings and not internalize them.

"It's Natalie. She's dead."

"She's not dead. I just saw her six days ago. Remember, I told you about how John and I went to make sure she was doing all right. Then I tried to have drinks with her three days ago. She didn't stay, though. Honestly, she didn't look great. I'm not sure that she was all right mentally. But, she definitely wasn't dead. AND, more importantly, I received a voicemail from her yesterday. She wants to meet for drinks."

"Alice, you aren't processing what I'm saying. I am telling you that she's dead. Natalie's mother called me. I was going to take the day off, but I needed to tell you. Why don't you come with me? We'll have some tequila shots or whatever the fuck shots and I can tell you the whole story."

"It's eight thirty-three in the morning," Alice responded. "It's too early to drink."

"It's not too early to drink when one of your best friends is dead."

"Luckily, that isn't the case."

Ryan put his hands on Alice's face. One on each side of her cheek. And forced her to look him in the eye. "I need you to listen to the words coming out of my mouth. Natalie is dead. Her mother is coming down to ID the body. I'm going with her this afternoon, so she has someone to lean on."

"Natalie's dad died from a heart attack last year," Alice stated.

"That's true. That doesn't have any bearing on this current situation. You still aren't listening to me. As much as I hate to suggest it, do you want me to call John?"

"Why would you call John?"

"Alice. I need you to listen to me. Natalie is dead."

"She's not dead. I saw her last week."

"I'm calling John. Why don't you sit down." It was a statement, not a question.

Alice sat in the chair. She hadn't even made it to her office. She was sitting out in the middle of the lobby area. She felt random people putting their arms around her, but she didn't react. She didn't reciprocate any movement from the well-wishers who came to her. Each of them murmured words Alice couldn't comprehend.

It didn't matter. She sat in this chair. It had wooden arms, a soft seat, and a mesh back. The fabric green. She estimated it was eighty-five percent through its usable life. Perhaps, too many people had sat in the seat because it seemed well-hollowed in the center. Like someone larger than she had spent an extensive amount of time on the chair in question without regard to what that amount of bulk would do to a chair of this size. Very irresponsible, Alice thought. People could be very careless with others' things.

John appeared later. A little later. Much later. Alice didn't know. "Alice, look at me, sweetheart." Alice looked over. John was on bended knee just as he had been when he proposed. "I need you to tell me what you need."

"Can you find Natalie? She'll know what's wrong and what to do."

"No, sweetheart, I can't. Natalie is dead. She died. Yesterday afternoon sometime. That's what Ryan said."

"Natalie wouldn't just die. I know she is mad at me. I don't know why. She wanted to tell me something. I think I know," Alice looked at John, troubled. "Do I know why she is mad at me? I'm sixty-five percent sure I know why she's mad at me."

"It's hard to know why women are mad or happy from one minute to the other," John equivocated. "Why don't you come with me? I've called your therapist and she pushed through a couple of pills of valium for you. We'll pick them up on the way home."

"I feel fuzzy. I don't need any more meds," Alice said. "Someone said that Natalie died."

John sighed, "Natalie died. Someone killed her. I'm worried about how you're handling this. You have a fragile constitution."

"I don't understand how someone could kill Natalie, when we just saw her a few days ago. We spoke to her. She was all right."

John picked her up out of the chair and held her like he was rocking a baby. "We're going home." He stared down at all of the people gathered around his wife. Some trying to help. Some incapable of passing up drama. "All of you go away. There's nothing to see here. I need to get my wife home." He sent a nod in the direction of the head of the department. "My wife will be taking a week off. I assume you can make that happen without any issues."

"Yes, sir," Alice's boss responded. "Take all the time you need."

With that answer, John carried Alice out of the building. He carefully placed his bride of ten years in the passenger seat of the car. He pulled the seatbelt and fastened it securely around her.

"Why are you still driving a rental?" Alice asked.

"It's a long, very unimportant story. Jessie is taking care of it. What's important is for you to be calm and feel better."

"Ok," Alice agreed amiably.

"Jessie is picking up your meds and will bring them to the house. Everything is fine."

"Do you think Natalie is dead?"

"Yes, sweetheart, I do."

Alice processed this answer for thirty seconds. "She was my best friend," Alice looked at John wondrously. "How can she die? She's not supposed to die. That's not what happens to regular people. We're regular people, aren't we? AREN'T WE?"

John hadn't started the car yet. "I think we're far from 'regular' people. But, no, Natalie wasn't supposed to die. What do you need from me? What can I do for you?"

"She's not supposed to be dead," Alice repeated. "Make her alive. You said you would do everything that I ever needed. This is what I need."

"Of all the things that I would do for you, of all the world that I would give up and change for you, this is the one thing I can't fix. I can't make this better. Close your eyes. I'll make you some tea when we get home. Later. A little later. Much later. I asked Jessie to pick them up. Once Jessie brings them to the house, I'll crush the pills in the tea. That way, you shouldn't taste them. I know you hate any bitterness."

"Thank you, John. I don't know what I would do without you. Please don't tell my parents I'm having issues. You know how they are."

"I will always take care of you. I'm always here for you. Always. I hope you know that," John said. "Just make sure that you always listen to me. The easiest way for me to protect you is for you to listen to me."

Chapter Thirty-four

Jessica

essica returned from checking on John's car at the body
shop. As she expected, they were more than happy to take
the cash and repair it. No questions asked. They even
gave her a better deal on it. The shop needed a few more
days to get the part in, but promised it would be done within
the week.

She was taking care of some miscellaneous errands for
John. He had called her cell yesterday evening. "Jessie, I need
your help. Alice is having a mini-breakdown and I need to
deal with it."

"What happened?"

"One of her friends was killed suddenly by a hit and
run."

"Oh no! What happened? Was the person drunk? Have
they found him?"

"We don't know. It happened in broad daylight. I would
kill the person who did this. For Alice," John said.

"Can I help?" Jessica asked.

"I need you to pick up some meds for my wife and drop them off at the house."

"Not a problem. Just let me know what pharmacy. Is there anything else you need? I'm at your disposal," Jessica said.

John rattled off a list of errands for her to complete, including picking up his dry cleaning. "I know some of these are more personal in nature and don't fall within your job description, but I don't know who else to call right now. I'm taking a few days off work to deal with Alice. I really need you right now. I'm sorry to keep repeating that. Everything is so crazy right now. I need one thing to be good. One person to be good."

"I'm happy to do what I can. How long do you think you will be out? Do you need me to arrange for meals? I can cook and drop some off if need be."

"Three days max. I have to get to work on that huge criminal case again. Now is not a great time to be missing work, what with the trial looming. If you could drop off dinner or go grocery shopping, that would be amazing. I'll leave a key under the rock in the front yard. The rock is off to the right and a little differently shaped," he stopped. "I might need to put Alice in the hospital. She isn't responding well to the news. If she can't accept her friend's death, it would probably be a seventy-two-hour hold. You don't know how difficult it can be, when Alice gets a little out of line."

John continued, "Also, if you don't mind keeping the reason why I'm taking a few days off on the hush-hush. The woman who died was the soon-to-be ex-wife of a close family friend. Her husband is fairly well-known in legal circles. The partners knew we were friends and assumed that's why I needed time. I don't want them to know that Alice is fragile. It doesn't look good for me."

"Your secrets are always safe with me. If you think of anything else you need, just send me a text."

Jessica heard a crash in the background. "I have to go. Alice, please stop throwing things..." John hung up the phone.

Jessica looked through the remaining list that she had created for John. She looked forward to grocery shopping and putting a few meals together.

*   *   *

She had spent about three hundred dollars on groceries. Probably a little overboard, but John was worth it. She paid for them on her credit card and placed the receipt into petty cash. It would help offset the money she had taken to fix the car. No one would question groceries for a bereaved member of the firm.

She busied herself around John's kitchen. The key had been easy enough to find in the yard. She found a pretty yellow apron with frills on it and didn't hesitate to strip naked, pull it over her head, and tie the strings behind her back. She had purchased flowers at the market and placed them in a dusty vase she had found in a cabinet.

She was marinating steaks and had a baked potato in the oven when she heard John's car pull into the driveway.

"Hello? Who's there?" John called out.

"It's just me. I was getting dinner together," Jessica said.

"I thought you were just going to drop off food in the fridge. You really shouldn't be here. Alice could have been here."

"I thought you would prefer my cooking to throwing something in the microwave. If Alice had been here, I would have just dropped everything off with instructions. I assume that because she isn't here that she's in the hospital?"

"Yeah. I called her father and we agreed that a commitment would be the best course of action." John loosened his tie. "I'm not sure what you're doing in my wife's apron, but I can't pretend that I'm not happy to see you here making dinner."

Jessica massaged his shoulders. "Leave everything to me. Can I pour you a scotch?"

"That would be amazing."

"Is Alice okay at the hospital?"

"I guess. I should have suspected that her meds weren't right. She has been acting a little paranoid and stand-offish for a while. I just haven't been paying enough attention to her, I guess."

"John, look at me. You can't blame yourself for your wife's illness. Was she sick when you married her?"

"Probably. It would make sense. I always wondered how it was so easy for me to marry a high society girl. She should have been swept up soon after she turned eighteen. It's the way mergers work in those families. I can only assume that people who ran in those circles knew she wasn't quite right. Her parents were beyond happy to have me in the family and for me to take Alice of their hands."

"She told you she needed meds every day before you got married, right?" Jessica badgered.

"I didn't know she was mentally unstable until the first time I put her in the hospital. I asked her dad about it then. You know what his answer was?"

"What?"

"Don't take her to the hospital. We have money and a facility that will house her correctly. Here's the number of the doctor we like and the number for the facility. The facility is quiet and knows how to keep things private. He said it like it's no big deal and it happens all the time. He told me to get used to it because it was my job to take care of Alice," John said. "How much longer until dinner?"

"Oh, let me check on the potatoes. Do you want me to grill the steaks or pan fry them?"

"Woman. Don't you know that only a man can be in charge of the grill?"

Jessica laughed and punched him in the arm. "Sometimes I forget."

When John burned the steaks, she told him, "These steaks are amazing. Perfectly cooked."

When they finished dinner, he turned on some old-school R&B on the radio and they danced around the house. Eventually, finishing in the bedroom.

John nuzzled her neck. "We shouldn't be doing this, but I need some comfort right now."

"Oh… John," Jessica sighed. "This is just deliciously bad. Delicious."

After sleeping beside him in his bed, Jessica woke before him. She got up and made coffee and threw together a quick breakfast.

John walked into the kitchen naked and with tousled hair. "What is this? I never get breakfast in the morning! I usually just get to clean up whatever ridiculously sad attempt Alice has made to leave me something to eat."

"A man needs to start his day off right," Jessica said.

They spent the next two nights in much the same way. On the third night, John said, "The funeral is tomorrow. I'll be picking Alice up from the hospital to go there. Then taking her home."

"I understand," Jessica stated. "I'll go ahead and wash the sheets and get them ready for her."

"Jessie, you are a wonder."

Chapter Thirty-five

Alice

"Alice, please. Everything is fine. Stop asking questions. Yes, I went grocery shopping, so there is food in the house. Yes, I cleaned the house. Yes, I know where the funeral home is." John sounded exasperated.

"I just need to know. I'm sorry. I'm not trying to be difficult," Alice said in a small voice.

"I know you aren't *trying* to be difficult. And yet, here we are."

"I'm sorry. I'll be better. I promise. I'll be better. Did we send flowers?"

"I arranged for flowers to be sent." John looked as if he were mentally applauding himself for that small feat. "We also donated to a scholarship fund that has been set up in her name."

"What's going to happen to her children?"

"I guess they will stay with their dad. I didn't ask."

"Oh." Alice slipped into the fall jacket that John held up for her. John checked her out of the facility and held a hand on her lower back to direct her towards the car.

"Is this still the rental?" Alice asked.

"Yes. Long story. But the bumper fell off after they fixed it."

"Oh, jeez. I can call them for you."

"Jessie already took care of it. Don't worry about it."

"Oh, Jessie took care of it," Alice repeated. She shook her head, trying to clear it. Her head still felt muzzy. There were some dots she needed to put together.

"Natalie's funeral is today," Alice said.

"Alice, that's where we're going. Are you ok? Are you sure that you want to do this? I understand if you aren't up to it."

"Of course, I do. I'm fine. You just overreacted. I didn't need to have that short stay in the facility. I was fine. I am fine."

John sighed and didn't answer.

They drove in silence for the next twenty minutes until they arrived at the funeral home.

The service started on time. Alice ignored most of the religious rites and passages. They held no meaning for her. She was sure the rites held no meaning for Natalie's body lying in the coffin.

When Ryan began the eulogy, Alice felt herself tear up. She bowed her head and listened to the words describing her friend wash over her. She felt the words trying to put a salve on her soul. She felt she might let them.

When the service was over, she looked towards the back of the room. Jessie was standing there. Alice felt cold. She nudged John in the side. "Is that Jessie?"

"Where?"

Alice nodded her head in the general direction.

"Are you sure you feel ok? Jessie's not there. Let's skip the graveside service and get you home. You need to rest," John said.

"No."

"Alice," John took her by the elbow. "We need to go. You aren't well."

"No. No. No. No. No. No," Alice began to screech and couldn't stop herself.

The other mourners openly stared at her. "Everything's ok. She's just having a hard time," John called out. In Alice's ear, he whispered, "Stop this right now. I'm taking you home. Stop this right now." Alice heard the impatience in his voice. He hated looking like he wasn't in control.

"No. No. No. No. No," she continued.

John picked her up. "Excuse me. Excuse me," he rammed through the tiny crowd with Alice in tow and put her in the car. He buckled her up. "What is wrong with you?" he seethed. "Why can't you just be normal? I just want to have a normal life. I don't want my whole life to be about taking care of you."

He stopped and rubbed his face. "I'm sorry that was cruel. I don't mean to be."

"I just want to go to the graveside service," Alice demanded.

"We went to the church service and now we're going home." He shook some pills that she recognized as Valium into his hand. Grabbing an old bottle of water that sat in the cup holder, he handed them both to her. "Take these. You aren't in any state to continue anymore. Just trust me. This is what you need."

Alice dutifully took the pills. "I don't see why we couldn't go to the burial site," Alice pouted.

"Because you're seeing things. That's not a good sign, Alice."

Alice passed out on the drive home. John somehow managed to get her into the house and into the bed. He took off her socks and shoes and didn't bother with anything else.

Alice thought she smelled a strange perfume in the pillows and the sheets. She must be smelling things, too.

As John said, hallucinations weren't a good sign.

Chapter Thirty-six

Jessica

Jessica sat in the back of the small funeral home. Very few attendees. Fewer flowers. Natalie McInroe was not a very important woman to anyone. She had no business trying to mess with John's life.

She listened to the preacher's monotone voice with the usual scriptures. She listened to the man; presumably, a friend of Natalie's, cry his way through some mundane words. She idly wondered why the jilted husband wasn't giving the eulogy. She thought that just for the purposes of helping his children cope with their mother's passing, he should at least give a small semblance of support. Ultimately, it wasn't her problem.

As she got up to leave, she found herself looking into the eyes of Alice Smith. She ducked behind a pillar and walked quickly away. It would not do for John to see her here. Not when they were on such good terms right now. Not when he was finally beginning to see precisely what Jessica could offer him.

Stability.

Love.

A woman who could take care of all his needs.

Alice couldn't provide anything for him. She was weak.

Jessica began to plan for the life that she and John would have. The life that would occur when Alice was gone. The life Jessica was due.

The phone rang. John's number. He stated without preamble, "Alice thinks she saw you at the funeral. That's not true, is it?"

"Her friend's funeral? Why would I be there? Can I help you? Do you need me to pick up more groceries?" Jessica spat out a bunch of questions.

"Everything's fine. No problems. Alice must have seen a ghost," John sounded like he was reassuring himself.

"I assume Alice is safely back at home?"

"Yeah. She's asleep in the bed."

Jessica thought about what had occurred in that bed and smiled. "I hope you think about me, when you see her there."

"Don't be disgusting."

Affronted, Jessica said, "How is that disgusting? You were there, too. I know you enjoyed it." She laughed throatily, "I could feel you enjoying it."

"I think this last week might have been a mistake. I'm not sure we should keep seeing each other. I need to focus on my wife," John said.

"No, it wasn't a mistake. It was what you wanted. I know you're super stressed out right now. Don't worry about it. I can wait for you until you're ready to see me again."

"Jessie, I need to think about what the best thing for me is right now. Please hear what I'm saying. I'm not leaving my wife. I need you to understand that." He paused. She didn't try to fill the emptiness with words. "Jessie. I'm. Not. Leaving. My. Wife."

John hung up the phone without saying anything else.

Jessica smiled to herself. She knew that no matter what John said, it would only be a matter of time before she and John were together.

Alice would be out of the way. Jessica would make sure of it.

Chapter Thirty-seven

Detective Morrison

Morrison sat by himself in the very last pew of the church. There were only about twenty people in attendance. Most of them seemed to be direct family or friends of the children. Morrison watched two young weeping children sitting in the front row next to a man who remained stoic, except for the angry stares at John Smith. Morrison assumed that was Natalie's husband. The one who threw her out and denied her access to her children. Morrison shook his head. And now, she would never be able to repair the relationship with her kids. Hopefully, the man felt proud of himself.

While the preacher recited soft platitudes about the nature of death and a higher plan, Morrison scanned the rest of those present. Over to the upfront left, he saw Alice and John Smith. Alice Smith wept openly. John Smith periodically handed her tissues, but mostly just looking bored.

Morrison thought John Smith should at least pretend to care. He should have the courtesy to look at least mildly remorseful that his former mistress had been splattered all over a street.

In fact, John Smith should be channeling all of his power to not look guilty. Natalie's death took care of all of his problems. A little remorse might have gone a long way towards clearing Morrison's suspicions that Smith had taken care of his problem personally.

Morrison made a mental note to ask Smith where he was at the time of her death. Smith better have fifteen witnesses and a DNA sample to prove his alibi. Everything seemed too neat. And too pat.

Smith would walk away without his wife knowing about his little Natalie problem. Natalie's death helped Smith out in the marriage department.

Morrison glanced to his left. A thin, blonde woman with a pinched face stood next to a pillar. Her manner of dress much too corporate looking for a funeral. She didn't make any movement to sit down. She just continued to observe the funeral from the back. Her behavior raised Morrison's hackles and he decided to speak with her after the funeral. There was something just odd about her presence and her demeanor. Morrison's mind couldn't quite tick it off, but something odd.

The preacher ended his sermon. A man stood up to do the eulogy. Morrison noticed that it wasn't Natalie's husband. Nor had the man made any movement to try to say anything.

"My name is Ryan Johnson. Natalie is…was…I'm sorry," the man held up a finger to ask for time to compose himself. "Natalie was one of my very good, very dear friends. I just wanted to say a few words about her to those who knew her and loved her."

Morrison sat up and paid attention. He wanted to learn more about Natalie from those who knew her best and loved her.

"Natalie was always too serious. She carried the weight of the world. Someone has to, I guess. But, that's a lonely way to live. I was happy to be one of the people Natalie confided in and could help her roll that stone up the hill for a minute," Mr. Johnson paused.

Morrison reflected on the time he had spent with Natalie. She was special. Special in a way that he hadn't seen in a long time. Special that made him laugh. Special that made him think. Special that made him miss what they could have been together.

He had made plans that included her.

Chapter Thirty-eight

Jessica

essica watched John reach for his pants and pull them on. Undershirt next. Dress shirt buttoned on top of that. It wasn't until he was tying his shoelaces that he looked up at her. "Jessie, I think we're done here."

She looked over at him from her position in the bed. The covers on the other side still pleasantly mussed.

"I know. It's time for you to head home to your wife. I really wish you would stay. Maybe you could get away on a work trip or something? I would love to see the leaves in New England this time of year. Maybe stay at a bed and breakfast?" Jessica asked. She had gotten out of bed to rub John's shoulders. She could feel the knots underneath the muscles.

"See, that right there is the problem, Jessie. We aren't going to go on vacation together. I tried to explain it to you before. This isn't a relationship. You just don't want to hear that."

"Ok. I understand. We can do something else. Maybe go to a nice restaurant. We don't always have to do carry out or eat in. Or, I could cook for you at your place. I enjoyed taking care of you at your home."

"No, absolutely not." John paused. "Jessie, you need to listen to me. Listen to what I'm saying. This was the last time. We can't see each other anymore. I've arranged for you to get another job. I would like you to clean out your desk and start at the new firm on Monday. I'll make sure that you get a nice severance package. The attorney who is taking you in is a very nice older gentleman."

He stood up and pulled a rectangular object out of his coat pocket. "I bought this for you as a symbol of our relationship. I hope you like it. I wanted you to have something to remember me by."

Jessica opened the box and found a gold sapphire bracelet interlaced with diamonds. "What is this?"

"I remember one time that you told me you like sapphires. I hope you appreciate it."

"What are you saying?"

"We are done. You need to move on. I need to focus on my wife. My wife is distraught. I'm worried about her mental health. It doesn't take much to throw her off the rails. She needs me," John said.

"I need you."

"No, you don't. You don't have any allegiances to me, nor I to you. Why can't you understand this? We're done. I'm trying to make this as easy as possible for you."

"What changed? What changed so much that you are willing to leave me behind? Is this about the funeral you accused me of stalking?"

"Stalking? I just asked if you were there. My wife thought she saw you. You know a…friend of mine was killed a few days ago. We weren't that close, but she and my wife were best friends. I just really need to think some things through."

"Natalie. That was the name of the woman who died, right? Natalie."

"How do you know that?" John asked.

"Because I love you. I know everything about you. I knew that Natalie was causing you some problems, so I helped you."

"What's that supposed to mean? You helped me." He paused, "Jessie, what did you do?"

"I took care of the problem. I did it for you. I knew she was making you unhappy. You seemed so grumpy lately, so unlike you. Natalie's the one who vandalized your car. I saw her doing it. I recognized her from your office appointment with her. I didn't tell you, because I didn't want you to be upset. Everything I do is for you. So that we can be together," Jessie stood up and went to kneel before John. "Everything I do is for us."

"Umm…ok. I'm still not sure what you are trying to say," John said.

"For you, I took care of the problem for you." Jessica reached for John's hand.

"What problem?" John asked.

"Natalie. I took care of Natalie for you. So, you can be free."

He pulled away from her. "Jessie, please don't be saying what I think you're saying."

"Why? You knew it needed to happen. You won't report me to the police, will you? I know this is what will bring us together."

"I never asked you to do this. I can't believe you would. I was going to pay Natalie off. That would have solved the problem. She would have left the city."

Jessica could see John working through the information she had given him. She watched and waited for him to come to the obvious conclusion that they could be together. That Jessica was removing all obstacles for him. There was only one more obvious issue.

"When do you want to leave Alice? Where will we go? Somewhere warm, I hope." Jessica took John's limp hands between hers and held them to her heart.

"I need to go," John sounded shocked.

"I know this is a lot to process, but I love you so much. I hope this proves that I will do anything for you. That I'm the one you need to be with. The only person you can trust."

"I understand everything that I need to know," John said. "I have to go. I need to talk to Alice."

"When will you be back?" Jessica asked.

"When everything is ready to go." John looked upwards and to the left as he spoke. He took his hands back and made a process of straightening his shirt. "Just do me one favor, please. Stay home, while I get all of this worked out. You're right. I was planning on leaving Alice for you, but I need a few more days. Will that be ok?"

"Of course! I'll do anything you want. I'm so excited. Do you want me to arrange anything?"

"No," John answered quickly. "No. Let me do everything."

Chapter Thirty-nine

Alice

"I don't understand why you want to have dinner with my parents. You know they make me crazy," Alice said.

"Sweetheart, we haven't seen them in a very long time. It's good to keep up relations. Besides, I have some things I need to talk to your father about."

"What do you need to speak to him about?"

"Business things."

"You're being strange," Alice commented.

"Maybe there are just some things that I want to talk to your dad about. Maybe I have a little surprise up my sleeve," John winked. "Oh, don't wear that dress. Wear the light blue one. It looks a lot better on you. You've lost a lot of weight recently. Are you sure you don't want to call someone in to do your hair?"

"Do you think I should?" Alice asked.

"It would just be easier for you. I know how much your parents stress you out."

"Ok. That's fair. But, I'll go into the salon. I hate it when people come to the house."

"Sounds like a perfect plan."

Alice went about setting up her hair appointment. It was odd that John had suddenly decided to have dinner with her parents. Very last minute. She couldn't remember him ever doing that before. She hated that they were coming to her home where she and John lived. Where she felt most comfortable in her skin.

She made some quick arrangements to get a last-minute chef. She knew John wanted to host the dinner at the house, so he and her father could retire to the study. To talk about whatever men talk about when they drink copious amounts of scotch and the women are gone. Leaving Alice to listen to her mother all evening rehash Alice's mistakes regarding dinner and likely her entire life.

The doorbell rang. "Good afternoon. I'm Chef Brian. I'm here to prepare a meal for four this evening at six. I would like to get started prepping the food and get an idea about the layout of your kitchen. I want to make sure everything is perfect."

Alice waved him in distractedly. "Yes, yes. Let me show you where everything is. I'm running out for a hair appointment in a few minutes. Just use whatever you need. We'll be eating in the dining room. Did you bring the appropriate wine to pair with the meal?"

Chef Brian nodded affirmatively.

"Thanks. I'll be back soon." Alice grabbed her purse and walked out the door.

*   *   *

"How long has it been since you've been in? Look at these roots! How much time do I have to tame this wild mane?" her stylist clucked.

"About two hours. I have to get back for a dinner party. I'm the hostess this evening for a dinner my husband sprung on me."

"Hmmm…we will just have to do what we can. Have you seen the latest breakup for Justin Beiber? That boy…" Alice listened to her stylist prattle on. Relaxed in the sense that she wouldn't be expected to keep up her side of the conversation so she could focus on possible dinner topics with her family. She liked to have at least five different points to distract her mother from whatever complaint her mother would have regarding Alice that day and to entertain her father.

Point one. The weather. This was always an excellent topic to ease into a conversation. Especially since it had been neither too hot nor too cold. Very difficult to criticize.

Point two. The Democrats. Alice didn't care about politics herself, but this would enrage her father, who would dominate the conversation for at least thirty minutes.

Point three. The stock market. Another topic that her father would discuss at length. Generally, in relation to the Democrats ruining the country.

Point four. Upcoming Junior League Ball. Her mother was the chair. This one was a little dangerous because she didn't want her mother to volunteer Alice for any sort of committee.

Point five. Her neighbor's overgrown hedge. This would anger both her mother and father. Both felt it an affront for someone to live in a perfectly nice neighborhood and not hire an appropriate gardener.

These topics should get her through dinner. If Alice was lucky, they would even get her through the requisite after-dinner glass (perhaps glasses) of wine with her mother.

"Voila. You look beautiful as always!" Her stylist turned her toward the mirror sideways, picking up a hand mirror so she could see the back. "Your dinner will be scrumptious. Have fun! Ta Ta!"

Alice paid and tipped the requisite twenty percent and slowly moved towards her car. She drummed her fingers on the steering wheel for three minutes before she sighed and put the car in drive.

*   *   *

"Alice, I'm so glad you brought in a chef instead of trying to cook anything yourself. I know you try, darling, but you just aren't that good at it. Now, personally, I would have used Chef Cathy. A woman just has a better touch at finessing a dinner party," Evelyn Patrick remarked.

Chef Brian's staff was cleaning up the remnants of the dinner table. The fresh floral centerpiece sat low enough to the table to not impinge on the conversation. Candles had been lit in several areas to provide a soft glow. Not much food remained on any of the plates, besides Evelyn's. Because as Alice's mother always stated, a woman should never allow a man to see her eat.

Alice and her mother had a glass of Riesling out on the balcony. While, as expected, John and her father retired to the study. Alice mentally prepared herself for her mother's litany of her current offenses.

Alice sat on the outdoor cushioned patio chair. Not paying attention to her mother, but still interacting as she had since childhood. "Yes, mother. You're totally right. It's my fault. I didn't think it through all of the way." As long as Alice said appropriate words at the appropriate time, she could almost go into a meditative state and think about everything that had happened recently.

"And you know, I wish you would do something about your roots…" her mother droned on.

"Mother, have you looked at me? I just went to the stylist this afternoon."

"Don't be sassy. I see what I see."

Alice stood up suddenly. "Mother, I'm sorry, but dinner didn't agree with me. I'll be back."

"That's what you get for hiring a substandard chef. I've never even heard of this Chef Brian. I wish you would just listen to me and my…." Alice walked down the hall towards the study and let her mother's voice trail away.

She put her hand on the study's doorknob. But paused as she heard her father's voice, "Explain to me exactly why I would help you?"

"This woman… this person is threatening our life!" Alice heard John exclaim.

Her father answered, "No need to get loud. These things happen. Especially to men like us. I can't tell you the number of times I've had to write a settlement check to a female who got too big for her britches."

Muffled noises that sounded like John. Not dissimilar to his nighttime snores.

"No, no. If you are going to pay someone off, it has to be worthwhile. Have you learned nothing?" her father asked.

Alice walked away from the door. Better not to overhear anything more.

She didn't want to know who her husband was paying off. Or why.

John cared for her. More than he cared for anyone else.

She shook her head to clear it.

She wouldn't listen anymore.

She wouldn't follow this rabbit trail. She owed that to her husband.

As well as faith and fidelity.

Perhaps, love.

Chapter Forty

Alice

"Hi Jessie," Alice said as she opened the front door to her home. "What can I do for you?"

"Is John home? He asked me to drop off some paperwork."

"Not at the moment, but I expect him soon. I'm having a glass of Saturday afternoon wine. I know it's naughty, but everything lately has been complete madness," Alice said. "Would you like to join me and wait for him? He shouldn't be too long."

"Are you sure? I wouldn't want to put you out. I know John wanted this paperwork this evening so he could work on it. It's completely my fault that it wasn't done yet," Jessie said.

"Of course. Please, come in. He's been working so hard lately. From what he says, you *need* to come in and have a glass of wine with me. You have been a Godsend to us during these difficult times. I hope he's giving you a vacation after all of these late nights at the office."

"It's my pleasure to help. Besides, I get paid by the hour. It will be nice to have a little extra money in my savings account. Maybe I will take a vacation. He is always researching new vacation spots for you two. I'm a little jealous."

"Awww... that's so sweet!" Alice exclaimed. "He claims that he has been looking into places, but I'm never sure. He keeps telling me that he's going to make it up to me for us having to skip out on our honeymoon." Alice pointed at the kitchen table and motioned for Jessica to have a seat. "Do you have a wine preference? I have a Pinot Grigio open. I prefer white wine in the afternoon to red, don't you?"

"Whatever you're drinking is fine," Jessie responded.

"Oh, I read a statistic once in a food magazine that seventy-six percent of people will just drink whatever the hostess is serving even if they would prefer something else. I really can open something else, if you would like?" Alice said.

"No, Pinot Grigio sounds great. How much longer until John gets home?" Jessie asked.

"Not too much longer. Not too much. This gives me a chance to catch up with the other woman in his life," Alice said.

Jessica looked stricken, "What?"

"You *are* his work wife, right?" Alice giggled at her own joke.

Jessica nodded conspiratorially. "You know, we *do* have to take care of our man. Where would he be without us?"

They talked for another fifteen minutes waiting for John. Making chitchat about John's quirks and foibles.

"Hello! I'm home! Alice, do we have company? I see a car parked in my spot. I had to park about a block away. I hate it when people don't respect the assigned spots. If I wanted to walk a mile every time I parked the car, I wouldn't have spent the extra money to ensure that we had two parking spaces," John bellowed down the hall.

"I'm in here, honey!" Alice called. "Jessie stopped by to drop off paperwork. I don't think she expected to be here so long, but we poured a glass of wine, and you know how we girls can be."

"Wait... who's here? Alice, come here, please. I need to speak to you."

Alice joined John in the living room. John rapid-fired questions. "What's going on? What is she doing here? What are you talking about?"

"Jessie came to drop off some paperwork that you asked for. What's the problem? I think it's sweet that she would take the time to drop it off on a Sunday," Alice said.

"The problem," John said, speaking through clenched teeth. "The problem is that I asked her to not ever come to the house. I fired her a few days ago. She has no reason to be here. None."

"You never told me that," Alice accused. "What happened? I thought that Jessie might work out. She seemed so nice and interested in the work."

"Alice. I don't know how to say this."

"Just say it."

"Jessie came on to me. She built this whole relationship between us up inside her head. I had to let her go. She started getting violent."

"Violent? How?"

John answered, "Forget it. Forget I said that. I guess it was more of a feeling that she was on the verge of getting violent."

"Why didn't you tell me?" Alice asked.

"I didn't want you to worry. I thought I had taken care of the problem. I'm worried that Jessie is obsessed with me. I promise nothing ever happened. I was just nice to her. I think she's lonely and just invented a relationship."

"Invented a relationship?" Alice repeated. "John, you should have told me! I let her in our house!"

"I know. I'm sorry. That's why I needed to talk to your father. I figured a man like that had dealt with these types of issues before."

"A man like that? What's that supposed to mean?"

"A powerful man. I'm sure he's had his fair share of women trying to get ahead and trying to blackmail him," John said. Alice looked unconvinced.

"Please, just go into the bedroom. I'm going to get rid of her," John commanded.

"Do you want me to call the police?"

"No, no. I think she will leave. I'll just explain to her again. I'm so sorry. I should have been honest with you. I just worry that these last few weeks have been hard on you. I don't want you to be more stressed out because I made a bad hire."

Alice began to babble, "Whatever you think is the right thing to do, John. I just really think that maybe we should get the police involved. If you're worried that she's dangerous..."

"Everything will be fine. I just want to protect you. Go into the bedroom. If anything bad happens, you can call the police on your cell phone. But, I really don't think you will have to."

"Ok," Alice kissed him softly on the cheek and walked towards the bedroom, away from Jessie. She stopped about halfway there and pressed her body against the wall. Alice could hear John from this position, but he couldn't see her. In case Jessie got violent, Alice wanted to be nearby. She held her cell phone in her hand, prepared to call the police.

"What the actual fuck are you doing here?" Alice heard John ask.

"You want me to be here. I know that you do. You love me," Jessie whimpered.

"You were drinking wine with my wife. Get out of here. Get out right now or I'll call the police." Alice heard the sound of the table moving and a glass breaking.

Alice ran into the kitchen and found John grabbing Jessie by the nape of her neck and forcing her towards the door.

"Alice, I told you to go into the bedroom. I will take care of this," John gave a curt nod of his head on every word. "Please. Just do as I ask."

"I heard the glass breaking. What are you doing? John don't hurt her. I'm calling the police."

John released Jessie. "Get out of here. Don't come back."

Jessie sobbed, "Why don't you love me? I did everything for you. Everything. You can't treat me like this."

John pulled her through the kitchen doorway and pushed her down the hall.

"What's happening? John, don't hurt her," Alice started dialing the emergency number.

"Put that down," John snapped. "Jessie, get out of here! Get the fuck away from my wife!" He continued to shove her down the hallway towards the front door.

Jessie kept sobbing, "I know you love me. I know you do. Love me, please."

John opened the door and pushed Jessie outside. He locked the deadbolt behind him. He went to Alice and pulled her into a bear hug. "I know that was scary. I'm so sorry." He lifted her chin so that he could see into her eyes. "Nothing ever happened. She just went crazy and imagined all kinds of things. Do you trust me?"

"Yes. Yes, I do."

"I promise on your life that nothing happened. I would never hurt you. I just want to protect you. Do you believe me?"

"Yes, I do," Alice responded, her face still looking troubled. Jessie was unhinged. She could do anything.

Internally, Alice vowed to make a police report tomorrow when John was at work.

Chapter Forty-one

Detective Morrison

"Detective Morrison? Detective Morrison? Hi, it's Alice Smith. Do you remember me? You helped us out with that vandalism case on my husband's car a while ago?"

Morrison looked up from the paperwork he was completing. The precinct was quiet today, allowing the woman to head unimpeded towards his desk. "Yes, ma'am. What can I do for you?"

"Something horrible happened yesterday. I'm not supposed to be here, but I'm just so worried. Oh, my goodness… John is going to be so mad at me. Maybe I shouldn't be here. Maybe this was a mistake," she said.

"Why don't you tell me why you're here and what happened, and we can decide if it was a mistake together?" Morrison said kindly.

"Yes. Yes. Ok. That makes sense. I just feel like the ground is tipping out from beneath me. Nothing makes sense anymore. Nothing."

"Start from the beginning." Morrison set aside his paperwork. Usually, he would have asked a uniform officer to deal with Mrs. Smith. He didn't have time for these emotional extravagances. He still had one possible murder on his desk and Natalie's hit and run.

He still didn't have any answers about Natalie's death. The package of Rolaids on his desk attested to his lack of answers and his lack of ability. His knowledge of Natalie started with the Smiths. He had no other leads at this point. The detective working Natalie's case had become tight-lipped when he found out about Morrison's budding 'friendship' with her. Morrison would listen carefully to Alice Smith and decide where on the suspect spectrum her husband fell.

He planned to find Natalie's murderer. He would.

"I don't know where the beginning is. My husband told me not to come."

"I gathered as much."

"Jessica Allen came to my house yesterday. I had a glass of wine with her. She said she was there to drop off some paperwork for John. That he had asked her to come."

"Okay."

"No, not okay. John came home." Mrs. Smith looked troubled. "That's my husband, you remember?"

"I remember." Too clearly, Morrison thought.

"He told me to go to the bedroom. He said he had fired Jessie. I call her Jessie. That's what John calls her," Alice rambled. "John said she shouldn't be at the house. I didn't go where John told me to and I eavesdropped on their conversation. I know that makes me a bad wife, but I was worried. Jessie kept screaming that she loved him. And that he loved her. He… He put his hands on her."

Morrison perked up. "How?"

"He pushed her. I ran back into the kitchen because I heard broken glass. Eventually, John was able to convince her to leave. He said it was nothing. And not to talk to the police, but I… I guess I don't know why I'm here. Has Jessie been in to file a report?"

Morrison frowned. "On what happened yesterday?" Mrs. Smith nodded. He tapped a few keys on his computer. "Nothing is coming up in an incident report. That's not to say that she won't come in later today or tomorrow. Was she injured?"

"Maybe. I couldn't tell. She was screaming. And crying. It was horrible. John denied everything. Denied everything. She seemed so sure, though. But, John wouldn't lie to me, would he? Odds are completely against him lying to me. Eighty-five percent odds against."

"Ma'am, I'm not following you. What was Jessie saying?"

"I told you already. She and John loved each other. That can't be true. Can that be true? He told me that she was just lashing out because he had fired her."

Morrison waited for her to finish speaking. "Mrs. Smith, what do you know about Natalie McInroe?"

"What? I don't understand what she has to do with anything. She was my best friend. And she was murdered. I think she was murdered. I'm seventy percent sure she was murdered."

"What do you mean, 'you think she was murdered'?" Morrison asked, holding up his fingers like apostrophes.

"I sometimes get confused about things that have happened. John usually explains things, when I get all mixed up. Sometimes I feel her right next to me. If I can feel her presence, then she can't be dead. Right? Right?!?" Alice became more and more agitated.

"I'm the detective on Ms. McInroe's murder," Morrison uttered the lie seamlessly. "Mrs. Smith, I'm going to ask you a question, and it's important that you answer me honestly."

"I would always be honest," she whispered.

"Did you know that your husband was having an affair with Ms. McInroe?"

Mrs. Smith slammed her hands into Morrison's desk and pushed herself away. Her face screwed up as if smelling shit. "No, she wasn't. She was my best friend."

"Ma'am, the vandalized car? Mr. Smith's car? Did your husband ever get the report for the insurance? I know you asked me for the report number a couple of times to file with them. Did you file with the insurance company?"

"I don't know. He was supposed to follow up with that. Getting the report was stressing me out, so he just took over. I'm sure he submitted it, because he said he would."

"Did you ask him to? Or did he just take over?"

"John knows me and he knows what I need. You don't know me. You don't know anything. Why are you lying to me? I know that the police lie. You're doing it now."

"No, ma'am. I'm not lying. She told me. I put it in my report."

"John said you never found out who vandalized the car," Alice retorted.

"That's a lie. Your husband is the one who gave me Ms. McInroe's name. And now she's dead. Do you know anything about that?"

"No. What. No. I'm done here. I made a mistake. I shouldn't have come here."

"You said Ms. McInroe, Natalie, was your best friend. What if your husband killed her?"

"He didn't. He wouldn't."

"He might have. You don't know what a man will do to protect his life. To maintain the status quo. To keep from being caught."

"Caught from doing what?"

"Mrs. Smith, have you been listening to me? Your husband had an affair with Natalie McInroe. That woman is dead. Explain to me what I'm supposed to think. Now, your husband has assaulted another woman that I suspect he was having an affair with. You've just about confirmed it by coming here."

"I have to go. You don't know what you're talking about."

"Mrs. Smith, I do know what I'm talking about. I have a feeling that I will be seeing you soon. I'll talk to Jessica Allen and see what she has to say about yesterday's incident."

"Forget it. Forget I was here. John was right. I should have just listened to him. I always screw things up, when I don't listen to him. I can't... deal. I am so confused. I don't even know why I'm here." She stood and turned on her heel to go.

"Ma'am, where was your husband Tuesday afternoon between two and four p.m.?"

"With me. John was with me."

"Somehow, I highly doubt that. Keep in touch."

Morrison watched Alice Smith walk out the doors. His intuition telling him that she knew more about the situation than she was letting on.

If she was giving her husband an alibi, then her husband was hers. And that didn't sit well with Morrison.

Chapter Forty-two

Jessica

"Young lady, I'm glad you decided to meet me. I wasn't sure if you would show up, which would make things much more difficult. I'm sure the promise of some money helped. My name is Daniel Patrick," he held out his hand to shake hers. Jessica sat across from an older man with a slight paunch and very little hair. "It's not exactly a pleasure, but sometimes things need to be done in person. Do you know who I am?"

"Your name sounds familiar, but I can't quite place it," she said.

"I'm Alice's father."

"Oh."

"Yes, oh."

"Do you know why I'm here?"

"Not really. I assume it's about Alice."

"Well, of course, it's about Alice. I wouldn't concern myself in your affairs, if it were about anything else. My daughter is an exceptional girl. She gets very agitated and wound up. Too emotional. Even for a woman, she's too emotional."

"I'm not sure what that has to do with me," Jessica said.

"Young lady, you don't look stupid. Please don't try my patience by sounding as if you are. I know you engage in some sort of arrangement with my son-in-law."

Jessica opened her mouth to speak. Before she could say anything, Daniel Patrick continued, "I don't need you to confirm or deny or to give me your side of the story. Quite honestly, I don't care what you have to say. My understanding is that you have been fired and your arrangement terminated. And yet, you still continue to show up to places like my daughter's house and make it difficult for everyone involved."

"I don't think you really understand everything that was happening."

"Of course, I understand. Girls like you always go after men with power. I've had my own issues with your type over the years. Let's just get right down to it. How much?"

"What?"

"How much? How much money do you want? I'm prepared to transfer money into your bank account right now. You just need to go away. How about a hundred thousand dollars? Would that be enough?"

Jessica was speechless. He was trying to buy her off. Just like John tried buying off Natalie. She was the idiot sitting in a coffee shop listening to her self-worth being valued.

"This isn't happening," Jessica said.

"Rest assured that it is," Daniel Patrick said.

"You can't buy me. I'm not a whore."

"Of course, you are. Don't be offended. All women are whores. It just depends on how we pay them. Some we marry and pay for them throughout our lives. And some we pay off in lump sums. It doesn't matter. Ultimately, you're all the same."

"I'm not a whore," Jessica repeated.

"Yes, sweetheart, you are," Daniel said patiently. "Right now, we are just determining how pricy you are. Please note that price does not necessarily correlate with class."

Jessica just sat in the chair.

"Fine. Two hundred thousand. This just shows how much I love my little girl," Daniel offered.

"You just called her a whore."

"No, I didn't. She's my daughter."

"So, the term whore is for everyone not related to you," Jessica replied.

Daniel Patrick raised his hand in a shooting gun motion. "That's the ticket."

"What if I told you that I don't want your money?"

"I'm not going to force you to take it. You *will* leave this town. I'm going to make some phone calls and no one in this city will hire you. I'm going to call your property management company and you're about to get evicted. If I can think of a way to swing it, I will have your bank accounts frozen. You *are going* to leave town. Trust me. The only question that remains is how much money you are going to take with you. Two hundred fifty thousand is my final offer."

"You're a pig."

"Name calling won't change the offer."

"I'm going to call John. I'm going to tell him everything that you just said."

"Please call him. It will save me time. I think he'll be upset that you didn't agree to one of the lower numbers. Because, John *will* pay me back. He owes me that and more for my silence."

"He knows you're here," Jessica said, defeated.

"Who do you think asked me to come speak with you? I didn't pull your name out of a magic rabbit hat. What's your decision?"

"I'll take the two hundred and fifty thousand. I can't believe this. I'll leave, but can I have a week?"

"I'm feeling very gracious, so yes, you may have one, emphasis on one, week to leave. I will check. Don't make me angry for being so generous," Daniel Patrick condescended.

"No, sir, I won't."

"That's a good girl. That's a very good girl." Daniel Patrick looked Jessica over from head to toe. "You know, I'd be willing to bump that number up a little if you'd like to accompany me around the corner. You're a very pretty little girl. I have a small apartment for such… activities."

"You're disgusting."

"Certainly. But, is that a no?"

Jessica considered the extra money. "Fifty thousand."

"Sweetheart, for another fifty thousand, you better live in my bed for the next week before you go. And do everything I want, no questions asked."

"No questions asked," Jessica agreed. "Anything you want."

*   *   *

"I can't believe you. I actually can't believe you. You sent your father-in-law to talk me into becoming his whore. You fucking pig," Jessica screamed into the phone.

"Jessica, calm down. I don't know what you're talking about," John said.

"I knew you would say that. I fucking knew it. I thought you were different. I thought I was different. It's all the same. Everything is still the same."

"If you don't start making sense, I'm not going to talk to you."

"I don't want to talk over the phone," Jessica whisper shouted.

"Where would you like to talk?"

"The coffee shop where I was supposed to meet Natalie and pay her off for you."

"Why there?"

"It seems apropos."

"Don't use big words and think they make you sound smart," John stated.

"Don't be a condescending asshole."

"It's my best trait," John smirked. "See you at the coffee shop in an hour."

"I'm not available in an hour," Jessica responded.

"Yeah, you are. If you aren't there, I'll expect you to be out of my life. I don't ever want to hear from you again." Jessica heard the phone click as John hung up.

*   *   *

Jessica waited at the corner table for about twenty minutes before John showed up. She started to gather her things to leave when she saw him walking in the door. He went to the counter and ordered a coffee. Black, probably. She knew what he liked. It was another five minutes before he slid into the chair across from her.

"You're late," she stated.

"You picked this out of the way place. I can't drop everything I'm doing just to come out here. What exactly do you want?" John asked.

"Why are you doing this?"

"Doing what?"

"Pretending like I don't mean anything to you. Paying me off to pretend like nothing happened," Jessica's mouth twisted into an unattractive grimace.

"I told you. I need to focus on my wife right now. I don't need more complications. You're supposed to be easy. Not another woman to placate. Just take the money and move somewhere else. You can start over. Find a nice man. Start a nice family. All of the things normal women want to do."

"I don't want those things. I want to be with you. Remember those days we stayed at your house when Alice was gone? Weren't those days the best you've ever had? Don't you remember them at night? Remember how we were together? We could be together. It could be like that all the time."

"No. How many times do I have to say this? No. I'm not going to leave my wife for you. I'm not going to repeat it. Take the money and leave. Or don't take the money, but you still need to leave. I don't want to see you again. Ever."

"I need to get my personal items from work," Jessica threw her head back, so her hair went over her shoulder.

"No, you don't. If those random bits of garbage are so important, I'll have them couriered to you. Give me your account number for me to wire the money you want." John stood up from the table, shoving it towards Jessica.

She got up and grabbed his hand. "Not like this. Please not like this. I'll do anything for you."

Fellow coffee drinkers started to stare in their direction. "Stop making a scene," John said through clenched teeth. "You only have two options. Money or no money."

Jessica sat back in the booth. "Money," she whispered.

"Fine. You'll have it by the end of the week." John left the coffee shop.

A woman nearby leaned over and said, "You don't need him. Let him go."

Jessica stared at her. "Why don't you mind your own business, you cow? You don't know anything."

"Honey, it's written all over your face. I know he was wearing a wedding ring and you aren't. There isn't much else to say. Let him go."

"Learn to mind your own business!" Jessica screamed.

"I was just trying to be helpful," the woman huffed.

"Nobody asked for your help." Jessica ran/walked out the coffee shop door.

John would not do this to her. He wouldn't get away with this. He would not treat her like a common whore to be dismissed whenever the allotted amount of time expired.

Chapter Forty-three

Alice

Alice sat at the kitchen table with her recipe books out, making a list of groceries for the following week. She glanced at her list: four onions, six Roma tomatoes, two potatoes, one green bell pepper, one red bell pepper, one bag of spinach, two steaks, one pound of chicken. She started to page through the recipe books again, looking for a nice dinner for John. She wasn't the best cook, but she wanted to make something nice for him. She had been challenging lately and he had been having to take on a lot of the routine errands she did during the day.

As she tapped her pen against her lips and considered a flank steak with chimichurri, her phone rang, showing an unknown, local number. Alice answered it, "Hello. This is Alice."

"Alice, this is Jessica. John's assistant."

"John's former assistant. You aren't supposed to be calling me. John wouldn't like it. He told me to stay away from you," Alice replied.

"I want to talk to you. To tell you something."

"You're a liar. I don't need to hear anything you have to say."

"John and I have been having an affair for a while. He loves me. He's going to leave you for me."

"Jessie, I understand that you *think* these things are true. They just aren't. John and I have spoken at length about you. You need to get help. Don't be ashamed. Sometimes, I need help too."

"I'm not a liar," Jessie replied.

"You are."

"I'm not sure you think that. You're still talking to me. You could hang up."

"I could hang up," Alice conceded.

"You won't, because you believe me."

"I don't."

"You do. That apron in your kitchen. The yellow, frilly one? I wore it in your kitchen while he pounded me from the back."

"You have a filthy, filthy mouth. Your mother would be ashamed of you," Alice said.

"She probably would be ashamed of me. I think she was ashamed of me, when she was alive. None of that changes the fact that John and I had an affair. He loves me, you know. He loves me. He's going to leave you for me. He will."

"My therapist is excellent. Do you want me to see if she has any openings?" Alice asked.

"You aren't listening to me. John loves me. He doesn't love you."

Alice snorted, "I'm done with this conversation. Jessie, I'm sorry that you are having emotional issues because you were fired. Making up stories isn't going to help you or anyone else. You helped John for a while, but it's time to move on and stop making up lies."

"How many times do I have to tell you that…" Jessie began, but Alice hung up on her. She didn't have time for this nonsense.

She went back to reviewing her grocery list. The chimichurri might be too crazy for John. He liked things to be more fundamental. To make sense. She flipped through a few more recipes and decided on a basic steak and potato dinner. That was more John. More of what he would like.

Alice put the remaining items on her list and left the house. She headed for the grocery store and put Jessie's phone call out of her mind. The woman was delusional. Alice didn't want to waste any extra worry on her. Alice wished her well, but Alice needed to focus on her own family.

Chapter Forty-four

Jessica

ies.

All of it. Lies.

Lies she believed because she wanted to believe.

That belief was broken. She remembered the careless way she had been treated. She only had to look at the blood under her fingernails to know her beliefs had changed.

*   *   *

Earlier, she had entered the house.

"Jessie! What are you doing here? How did you get in the house? You aren't supposed to be here." John walked towards her in the doorway. He sounded excited to see her, but unsure. His voice sounded loud and angry.

"You never changed the locks from when we spent our week together. I'm here because I wanted to talk to Alice again. I called her and spoke to her on the phone, but it isn't the same as face to face."

John's face turned stony. "When did you call her?"

"Just now. I told her everything. I'm not sure what she's going to do with all of the information."

"There isn't anything that you could have said to Alice that I haven't already told her. I'm not going to allow you to speak to her. I don't trust you with Alice," John said. "You need to understand fully and completely that I'm not leaving my wife. Jessie, there isn't anything between you and me. I've told you several times. It was an arrangement that worked well for a time. That arrangement is over."

"We've been to dinner together. You've bought me gifts. You've made love to me. I felt it! I felt that you loved me. It was real. I just wanted to talk to her and tell her it was time that she let you go. She seems confused," Jessica heard her voice rising and her words falling out of her mouth faster and faster. She could feel the blood rushing to her face. "I'm who you need. I do everything for you. It's what you want. All I want is to make you happy."

"I don't love you. I paid for dinner because that's how these arrangements work. I assumed, perhaps wrongly, you knew what you were getting into. I'm not going to leave my wife for you. I would never leave Alice for someone like you."

"You know that we did more than just have an arrangement! We danced together, slept together in the same bed. You love me! I fix your problems. It's me. I'm the one who takes care of you."

"I don't love you. What problems? I never asked you to do anything. Seriously, I don't… I don't know what you are doing in my house."

"You know why I'm here. Why are you pretending?" Jessica shook her head and made a face. "I came in using the key you left for me. The key you hid for me. If you didn't want me here, you could have changed the locks. You could have put the key elsewhere. You didn't. You didn't for a reason. You wanted me to come! You asked for me to come!"

"You've been in my home. Yes, when Alice was in treatment. You've lost your mind. Why won't you just take the money and run? Be normal. Understand where you are in the marriage hierarchy," John stated calmly.

Jessica moved to press her body against his. She whispered, "You know you want me. I can do more for you than your stupid wife ever could."

He moved and grabbed Jessica's shoulder and threw her against the wall. "You stupid bitch. I told you to never, ever under any circumstances come to my home. When I saw you sitting there with Alice. My god...what is wrong with you. You... you girls. You never understand. I'm not giving up my LIFE for you. You think I would leave my wife and my status for you? You girls are a dime a dozen. You're nothing. You need to understand that. You. Are. Nothing."

Jessica turned her head away while John ranted. She looked at a void in the upper right corner of the room, invisible to everyone except herself. She hadn't imagined their relationship. John cared for her, the way that she cared for him. She had just surprised him by coming to his house this way. A good surprise.

She bought groceries for him. She ran errands for him. She killed Natalie for him. Everything for him. No errand too small or too large. She would live for him. And only him.

John grabbed her jaw and turned her face towards him. She could feel his fingers dimpling her flesh. "You will look at me when I'm speaking to you," he stated through gritted teeth. He spat the next words in her face. "I. Am. Done. With. You. You are done. Don't come to my house. Don't show up to my office. I never want to see you again. Get the fuck out of my house. My wife is going to be home soon. You need to be gone."

"Your wife? Your wife? Are you kidding me? You don't care about her. You love me." Jessica fell to her knees sobbing. "I told her everything about us. You'll see. She hates you. She won't let you come back to her. You don't have any choice but to come back to me."

"You think you're the first girl to share my bed? The first one to think that I would leave my wife? To threaten me? Get out of my house. Get the fuck out. You're nothing. Nothing." John grabbed her arm and started dragging her towards the door.

"No! You don't understand! This isn't supposed to happen this way. I killed Natalie for you. She was going to tell your wife about the two of you. I solved the problem. Me!" Jessica kicked over a shelf containing all kinds of detritus from a peaceful married life. A pair of scissors fell out. Jessica grabbed them by the handle and thrust them into John's stomach. "You belong to me. Why can't you understand that?"

John's eyes grew large and round in surprise. "What the fuck is wrong with you? Why would you do this? Fuck. You fucking whore." He fell to the ground and tried ineffectually to grab the scissors from Jessica, all the while holding a hand to his stomach to staunch the bleeding.

She ignored his attempts to stop her. She ignored his dirty, nasty words. "Why," stab. "Are," stab. "You," stab. "Making," stab. "Me," stab. "Do," stab. "This?" stab. Each word punctuated with a bloody movement. Each stab ending in a punctuation mark on John's stomach, neck or face.

He was no longer moving. Not even a whisper of movement. She sat down beside him. Sobbing. Her shoulders shaking with grief. How did this happen?

How could this have happened again? And to her? Why did it always happen to her?

Jessica took a deep breath. She needed to compose herself.

She stood and looked at the blood that surrounded her. She wanted a piece of John to take with her. To remember the good times. Bending over, she used the scissors and took a few snips of his hair. She left the inferior lock of hair on the ground. The other she put in her pants pocket.

She saw a dish towel on the stove and began to wipe off the scissors. She laid them gently on his torn belly. She kissed his lips one last time and went through the hallway, carefully avoiding tracking any of his blood through the rest of the house.

On the way out, Jessica called his phone one last time to hear his voice. She waited for the phone to ring and heard it chime from his pants pocket. She pulled it out and held it in her hand as she left the house.

She needed to leave. Alice would be coming home soon.

Chapter Forty-five

Alice

A lice's mind churned through everything that had happened over the last month. Natalie's reluctance to continue being her friend. Ryan implying that John and cheated with Natalie. Jessie showing up at the house. Jessie fighting with John. Accusing him of having a relationship. Natalie dying. Jessie's phone call.

She had to confront John. She needed to know the truth. She needed to know if he had cheated on her. If he did cheat on her, had it been repeatedly? Was it her fault? Did she make John cheat on her with her constant mental issues?

Most importantly, she needed to know if she cared.

Did it matter? Did it affect her marriage?

She had watched her father have numerous relationships with other women. Surely her mother knew about them. Maybe marriage wasn't about love so much as it was about being with someone who protected you and supported you. Love could be secondary or even tertiary.

Maybe sex didn't have to be about love.

Marriage was John showing up at the hospital and sitting by her side. Holding her hand, when she didn't think she could go on. Taking care of her. Making decisions for her, when she couldn't be trusted.

She needed to know. Before she could decide on an answer to any of these questions, she needed to know.

Maybe. Maybe she needed to know.

Maybe, it was better not to know. If she knew, did she have to do something about the problem? Issue an ultimatum? Make him stop? Threaten divorce?

What if he left her?

What if she didn't love him?

What if she did?

"Self, I need you to take a deep meditative breath. Decide what you want to know before you get home. What can you live with? Is it better to be lied to and go on with your life? A life you could be happy with? Or, told the truth and just blindly look past certain things? Or, told the truth and have to leave John? The only man who has ever loved you," Alice said everything aloud. Hearing her own voice calmed her. Grounded her. "Would you be good with only seventy percent of his love?"

When it came down to it, she had two choices. Stay with John. Or, leave him. The thought of leaving him made her stomach gurgle uncomfortably and tears formed in her eyes.

The thought of staying with John calmed her. Comforted her in a way that nothing else could.

She would stay with him. But, she needed to know the answers to her questions.

She arrived at the house and sat in the driveway for about fifteen minutes. John didn't come outside to check on her.

She got out of the vehicle and went up the walkway to the front door. She noticed it was ajar.

"John? John? I'm home. Where are you? We need to sit down and talk. Really talk. I'm not happy with the way some things have been going. And I don't think that you are either."

Alice pulled her coat off and hung it in on the coat rack to the side of the door. "John? Can you hear me? I don't want to yell the whole time. I want to sit down and calmly have a conversation."

Alice entered the hallway. She tripped over something and bounced into the wall. "What in the...John? Why are you on the ground? What's happened? Are you okay? Should I call 911?" The questions kept pouring out of Alice's mouth.

She went to her knees and touched his face. It felt warm to her. She moved her tiny hands down the body she knew as well as her own. She searched for something her mind couldn't understand. Her eyes followed the path her hands trekked. She could smell something coppery. She felt something warm on her fingers.

"John? What do I need to do? John?" she asked. "John, I need you to move. Just a little bit. I'm not strong enough."

Water began to leak onto him. She touched her face with her fingers and realized the water was coming from her eyes. She looked to the side and saw a lock of his hair. Lying on the ground, next to his head.

"John. I need you to tell me what to do. I don't know what to do. I don't feel good. This isn't right. This isn't right. Tell me what to do. I need you. Please. I need."

She grabbed the lock of hair and held it to her heart. John still hadn't moved.

"John. This is not a good place to take a nap. And there are things all over the hallway. What have you been up to? I came all the way home because I need to have a conversation and here you are just lying in the hallway."

John's face remained remote and impassive.

"I need to take a vacation. I really do. I need to get my mind wrapped around some things. Then we are going to have a crucial conversation about the state of our marriage. I'm going to go pack."

John didn't get up.

"Don't try to stop me. I need to go by myself." She leaned down and kissed his face. The only movement was a growing pool of blood that he lay in. "John, I'm leaving. Are you ok? You're starting to scare me."

Alice stepped over John and went into the bedroom. She didn't see herself in the mirror or she might have changed the clothes that had John's blood all over them. She might have washed her face to remove the guilty trail her fingers had left. She might have seen the shocked expression in her eyes and called the police.

She packed one swimsuit, two sweaters, one T-shirt, four pairs of underwear, three bras, two pairs of shorts and six pairs of socks. Everything fit into a backpack.

As she walked out the door of her home, she dialed John's number. She needed to let him know that she would be taking a short vacation.

Chapter Forty-six

Jessica

"This is 911. What is your emergency?"

"I just heard a lot of screaming and crying coming from my neighbor's house. I think you should check on them. I was afraid to go over there," Jessica put a quiver into her voice.

"What's the address?"

"1221 Somerset Drive."

"What's your name?"

She hung up John's phone before giving any more information. The phone rang in her hand, she answered it without thinking. "Hello?"

"Hi…" There was a pause. "Jessie? Is that you?"

Jessica jerked the phone away from her ear. She looked at the display. It read wife. "Shit," she swore and pushed end. The phone began to ring again.

She flipped the phone over and took the battery out. No one would be able to ping the phone without the battery.

She remembered this from watching 60 Minutes or possibly a random blog. She threw the actual cell phone out the car window into a ditch. No one would find it. And, if they did, it would be unlikely that they would ever trace it to John. For all of the great crime-solving that the police did on TV, Jessica found that the police were not that competent in real life.

She drove back to her house. She would be leaving soon. She had all of that money from Daniel Patrick. It was nice that he paid upfront.

Maybe, she would go west. It would be nice to get away from all of the cold air. Arizona had a nice ring to it.

Chapter Forty-seven

Detective Morrison

"I need you to go to the crime scene of another body," Morrison's commander said.

Morrison threw down the pen he was using to correct a previous report. "Another? You have got to be kidding me. Seriously. This is a prank. I've asked this before, and I'm going to ask it again. Does anyone else in this whole fucking police department work? Am I Atlas holding up the thin blue line?"

"Calm down. You've already filed incident reports regarding the vic. John Smith. Had an anonymous 911 caller say she heard screaming at the house. Uniforms roll and there's a dead body inside. Door to the house left wide open."

"John Smith? What? How?"

"I guess we'll know the answers to those questions when you get your ass out of the chair and go check it out." His commander relented a little, "I know you have been getting a lot of bodies lately. I can see you've been stressed. I know the death of your friend, Natalie, didn't help. Even though I warned you about getting involved with her," the commander couldn't resist putting in a tiny jab. He continued, "If you want me to send someone else because you aren't capable of doing your job, I will."

"I'll go. I just… This whole thing is just crazy. I must have pissed off someone's god to be put right in the middle of this," Morrison said.

"Go. Figure this thing out."

Morrison went.

*   *   *

When Morrison arrived at the Smith house, organized chaos permeated the area. Patrol officers had roped off the area. Neighbors stood just outside the crime scene tape with their long giraffe necks swiveling. The coroner came on the scene about two minutes after Morrison. They nodded at each other as the coroner walked into the house. Surveying the area, Morrison followed him.

On the ground, evidence markers tagged bloody footprints. Morrison pointed at one and asked the nearest crime scene tech, "How many of these are there?"

"A lot. They go into the bedroom and out of it. Then they are pointed out of the house."

"Huh. Ok."

Morrison gave a cursory look at the body on the ground. He noted the blood soaking through the carpet and the numerous puncture wounds. Smith had been an asshole, but even assholes deserved a better death than this.

He followed the bloody footprints into the bedroom. A quick glance revealed the bedroom to be in disarray. Clothes all over the floor. A bottle of perfume lay broken on the ground. The lavender fumes mingled with the coppery scent of blood reached Morrison's nose making him want to retch. He left the room.

He approached a patrol officer. "Where's the wife? Alice."

"Who?"

Morrison rolled his eyes, "The wife. Alice. Where is she? Has she been contacted? These footprints look small."

"No one has called anyone. We were waiting for you."

Chapter Forty-eight

Alice

The last words that Alice fully registered and comprehended were Detective Morrison's: "This woman has been in and out of lucidity since we picked her up at the airport."

She eavesdropped distractedly as she waited for her attorney in a holding cell inside the police department.

They had taken all of her things. Her purse, her keys, the lock of John's hair.

They said she was fleeing the country after she killed John. A ridiculous thing for them to say. She would never do either of those things.

John. He would clear everything up. Especially when he turned up not murdered.

She needed to talk to him. "Excuse me, excuse me. I really need to speak to my husband. I've been waiting patiently, but I really need to speak to him now."

An officer sitting at a desk towards the back of the holding cells shook his head. "Lady, that's not going to happen."

Alice stood up. "John! John! Where are you? John, come help me, please. I need your help." Alice curled up on the floor sobbing. "John. Please help me, please. I'm ready to go. Let's go anywhere you want. Let's just go."

Time passed. Maybe ten seconds, maybe an hour. Alice didn't know. Her shoulders began to ache from being pressed into the hard floor. She had laid on the unforgiving floor, since she entered the cell. She tried to move, but couldn't will her body to sit up. Easier to just stay in her fetal position.

"Lady, your attorney's here. We're going to bring you into another room. You aren't going to try anything stupid, are you?" Alice just stared at the officer. "We're going to cuff you to make sure that everything stays just fine. Put your hands out." Alice just stared. She heard the words, but couldn't comprehend their meaning.

The officer sighed and called over his shoulder. "We're going to need a little bit of help here."

*　　*　　*

"Alice, sweetheart, it's good to see you. What happened? How did you get yourself into this mess?" Alice looked up and into the face of her family's attorney.

"I don't know what's happening. I'm so glad John called you. I'm just so worried. No one will tell me anything. I think something bad might have happened."

"Alice, John didn't call me. John's dead."

"No, no. He's not dead. I saw him at the house. I told him I was going on vacation, just like we always said we would. I'm ninety percent sure he isn't dead."

"When did you tell him this?"

Alice rolled her eyes. "At the house, I just told you. I told him at the house."

"Today?"

"Why aren't you listening to me. Yes, today. I came home early from work to talk to him and I told him I was going on vacation."

"Where was John?"

"Lying in the middle of the floor. He was exhausted, I guess, and couldn't make it to the bed. It's been a long couple of months for both of us."

"Alice, you aren't making very much sense. I really need to know what happened. Did you hurt John?"

"He hurt me."

"How? When? The police didn't tell me you had any marks or bruising."

"He had an affair, I think. I'm seventy percent sure. I'm ninety-five percent sure I love him, though. I wouldn't hurt him. Not like he hurt me. One hundred percent sure that I wouldn't hurt him."

"Alice, what are you saying? Did you hurt John? I need you to help me, so I can plan your defense."

"I didn't hurt *him*. He hurt *me*. You aren't listening. I went home to talk to John. I found…found I don't know what I found. I found a lock of his hair. I need his hair. Where is John's hair? We're going to Mexico. Did you know that?"

"Alice, I'm going to talk to the police. I need you to think about what happened today. I need you to tell me what happened."

"I told you John hurt me. I didn't hurt him. When do you think I'll be able to see him again? I haven't gone grocery shopping yet. We're out of triple cream brie."

"Ok, Alice. I understand." The attorney got up from the table and knocked twice on the door. It opened. "We're done here," he said. "Has this case been assigned a prosecutor yet, or who is taking the arraignment? I just want them to know I will be filing paperwork for a competency hearing and likely for insanity at the time of the offense, as well."

Once more, Alice was shuttled off to a holding cell. She laid down on the floor and continued to wait for John to come and get her. It shouldn't be too much longer. As soon as he heard she was in a jail cell, John would come running.

Chapter Forty-nine

Detective Morrison

M orrison kept his head down and kept typing on his report. The John Smith case. The dude was a piece of work and his wife was going to go down for killing him. Everything made sense.

History of cheating on the wife? Check.

Wife finds out? Check.

Dead body? Check.

Wife holding a piece of the husband's bloody hair? Check.

Blood found on her clothing? Check.

Wife trying to buy a ticket to Mexico just after killing him? Check.

The anonymous phone call bothered him. They couldn't track down the caller. All the call records revealed was a female voice. The number, itself, returned to Smith's own cell phone. But, why would the wife report the murder she committed? And then, do such a half-assed job covering it up?

Alice Smith couldn't even comprehend that her husband had died. Could she be capable of murder?

His next step would be to request call logs from the phone in question. He didn't expect it to return much. Based on his previous conversations with Smith, Smith had had several affairs in the past. Morrison expected some random numbers to be on there. Alice Smith didn't seem like the suspicious type, so there's no reason that Smith would have hidden anything.

But, this particular 911 call came from Smith's actual listed phone number. Not a random phone. Not a burner. *His* phone.

No name from the caller. No other information from the caller. Just a, "Hey, I hear arguing. Maybe you should stop in." It didn't feel right. More importantly, it didn't sit right in his gut.

The wife was a mess. Almost catatonic. If you asked her to add two and two, she would likely come up with six.

"Was this whole thing my fault?" Morrison asked out loud.

"What, Detective?" the officer sitting at the next desk over asked.

"Nothing. Just nothing. Talking to myself."

Maybe he shouldn't have told Alice Smith that her husband was cheating on her. Had been cheating on her for years. He could have told her about Natalie without divulging the affair. Maybe she would have found out anyway. The two had been friends for a long time, but maybe not. Natalie seemed firm on protecting Alice from any kind of emotional harm.

It just wasn't his place to tell a wife about her philandering husband, especially in a case that was just vandalism. He had let his own emotions, his blatant irritation with her husband, justify his actions. He had allowed his anger to overcome his common sense.

He opened the lower left-hand drawer of his desk. The last file tab remained unlabeled, but held all the cases that Morrison harbored doubts about. The prosecution didn't know about this file. He would lose his job if they did.

Sometimes, a case just didn't feel done and he wasn't ready to call it closed.

This one didn't.

Everything seemed too pat. Too perfect. Very few cases ever ended this perfectly. Fewer still finished with every string being bound up nicely in a bow.

He was missing something.

Alice Smith was right. Mexico did sound good this time of year. He could squeeze a short stay out of his meager paychecks. Life would be clearer after a vacation.

Maybe then he would take this case out of that unlabeled folder and feel good about the outcome.

Chapter Fifty

Jessica

"Alice Smith has been apprehended at the O'Hare Airport for allegedly murdering her husband. Police found John Smith, her husband, stabbed to death with a pair of scissors on the floor of the family home after receiving an anonymous tip. Mrs. Smith will face arraignment for first-degree murder in the morning. On a happier note, Lucky, the dog who went missing after his owner's tragic death, has found his family!" The newscaster continued to drone on about the lost dog that managed to make its way back home to its family after an entire month had passed.

Jessica watched the news coverage and clucked her tongue. Alice received precisely what she deserved. Like so many wives that took their husbands for granted.

After having a relaxing glass of Pinot Grigio, which Jessica had to agree with Alice, was a lovely afternoon wine, Jessica realized her thoughts of moving were simply ridiculous. She liked her home. She would just have to change jobs. Everything would be fine. Regardless of his boasts, Daniel Patrick couldn't have a stranglehold on the city's entire employment force.

Besides, she wanted to keep at least one eye on Alice. That woman was losing it. She looked crazy in the news report. Who knew what a woman like that could do? Maybe, Jessica would visit Alice at the jail. That would be the nice thing to do. Help her through this difficult time.

Looking through her updated resume, Jessica didn't see any mistakes. The correct dates for working with John were listed. She sent the resume to her printer. Time to find another job. Ho-hum.

Maybe this next time, it would work out. No more married men.

It always ended poorly.

She heard a sharp knock on her door. "Coming," she yelled absentmindedly. Looking through the peephole, she saw the apartment complex's security officer.

"Your car is parked in the wrong spot. We looked it up through the apartment applications. The renter is complaining. Can you move it?" he asked.

"Of course! I'm so sorry. I didn't mean to. I'll do it right now. I didn't mean to cause any trouble," Jessica said.

*   *   *

"I'm sorry it's taken me so long to come to see you. I'm glad to see that they have let you settle in at this facility instead of putting you in jail. I'm sure this is so much nicer than one of those jail cells," Jessica smiled softly.

Alice sat dumbly across from her. She had been moved to a psychiatric hospital after being deemed incompetent to stand trial. Jessica assumed Alice's father was paying the bill. This didn't seem like a state-run facility. It didn't smell like pee and mushed carrots for one thing. In front of Alice were colored pencils and a coloring page depicting a large parrot.

Jessica snapped her fingers in front of Alice's face. "Hello? Anyone in there?"

An orderly swiftly moved to Alice's side. "Ma'am, please don't agitate our neighbors."

Jessica laughed, "Your neighbors?"

"That's how we refer to our residents."

"I don't think Alice knows anything that's going on right now. You probably don't have to worry too much about her reporting you to your boss," Jessica said.

"All the same. I will cut this visit short, if you don't respect our neighbors and our rules."

"Yes, yes. Understood." Jessica waved him off. "Alice, I'm sorry if I offended you."

Alice continued to stare at her like a dumb cow. Well… no… not a cow. She was too frail and skinny. Jessica thought she could reach out and snap Alice's bird neck. Alice wouldn't make a peep.

"I suppose you're going to be here for a long time. You seem like you can keep a secret. Can you? I have some things I'd like to tell you."

Alice continued to stare vacantly.

"Oh sweetheart, you're drooling." Jessica pulled a handkerchief out of her purse and dabbed Alice's chin.

"I feel like it's important that you know I killed John. He was going to run away with me, you know. We were going to start a new family. We made love in your bed, when you were in the hospital. I told John I had changed the sheets, but I didn't. Shhh… don't tell." Jessica held one finger up to her lips.

Alice blinked once.

"You're such a good listener. Oh, Alice. I have a lot of secrets. Do you think that secrets can eat you up inside like a cancer? That once you have too many, they replace your innards and writhe like snakes in your belly?"

Alice blinked again. Jessica took that for assent.

"I've killed nine people in my whole life. Lovers who didn't deserve to continue forward in life. People who stood in the way of those that I loved and I believed loved me. I saved my little brother, though. Did you know I have a little brother? I don't tell a lot of people. I killed my mom and the kid's dad, but I saved him. I could have been hurt saving him. There was carbon monoxide all over the place, but I thought it was the right thing to do. The kid hadn't done anything wrong. He likely will in the future. That's what boys grow up to be. Men who carelessly throw people away," Jessica paused. "Maybe I made a mistake."

Jessica sat back in her chair and studied Alice. "I've heard that you can read someone's life through the lines on their face. You've had a hard life, Alice. The lines on your face make you look like an old woman. A woman for whom not much has gone well. I feel bad for making your life worse, but you didn't deserve a man like John. You really didn't. He needed me. He wanted me. You need to be here, because you stopped us from being together. If you think about it, you're the person that I should have killed. Everything would have turned out better that way, I think."

Jessica paused and wiped more drool off Alice's chin. Did she imagine it or did Alice's eyes narrow slightly?

Imagination. Alice wasn't capable of thought right now.

"The only time I've been in trouble was when I was a kid and killed my boyfriend's cat. I was so stupid back then. I don't know what I was thinking. I should have just poisoned the cat, but I wanted to be all hands-on. Thankfully, I learn from my mistakes. Do you learn, Alice? Have you learned from your mistakes? Would you still turn a blind eye towards John loving another woman?" Jessica said.

Jessica looked down at the table at Alice's perfectly manicured nails. "Looks like Daddy pulled out all the stops. Your nails look better than mine."

Jessica continued conversationally, "This is therapeutic. I'm glad I came here today! Maybe, I'll come back later. I'm sure you're going to be here for a very long time. Oh?" Jessica pretended that Alice had asked a question. "The third man I killed was my first lover. Men always pretend that they will leave their lives... ooops, I mean wives... for you. It's not true. I walked into a shared company apartment, because I saw he had an 'appointment.'" Jessica put her fingers up and put the word appointment in quotes. "I walked into this place, and the asshole was having sex with a random woman. Right in front of me. Do you believe it? Oh, and I guess the fourth person was that woman. Women can be forgettable."

Alice's hand twitched mildly.

"How? He'd taken me shooting several times. He thought that counted as a good date. He liked me so much that he gave me a key to the house. It was easier for me to get in and out that way. I knew he kept a handgun in his bedside drawer, and I went right to it. I shot them both while they were still both trying to cover up their nakedness. I kept the gun, though. It was one of my favorites. Light, but accurate," Jessica paused, closing her eyes and remembering the scene.

"The police are stupid. If you don't give them anything to go on, they can't solve anything."

Alice made a garbled noise. The orderly rushed over. "Is everything all right?"

"My old friend and I are just having a long-overdue conversation."

He chastised, "Well, don't upset her. It's almost time for her medication." The orderly walked away and sat in the corner. Jessica thought he seemed more interested than necessary.

"I killed my next lover. He had diabetes but was still very fit. I know you hear diabetes and you think an old, fat guy. But, no. Adam had it since he was a kid. I just switched out his insulin vials when he wasn't home. In a way, you could say he killed himself. He injected the insulin into his body. Watching him die will always be one of the great memories of my life," Jessica stopped talking. She twirled the ends of her hair and looked into the distance.

After a few minutes, she continued, "Then, of course, there was Natalie. I had to kill Natalie. She was screwing your husband. Did you know that? She was a little whore and then thought she could get money from John. I'm pretty sure he even gave her some money. Did you know that? I'm sure he didn't offer much. She wasn't worth much. Even that Detective Morrison was in on it. I found out that he covered everything up for her. Did you know that? I wonder if they were fucking. Ridiculous."

Jessica paused. "You already know about John. I'm only sorry about him because I thought we had a future. Can you imagine how beautiful our babies would be? It's really a shame."

Jessica stopped and looked out the window.

Alice garbled more words.

"I know, dear," Jessica said and patted her on the hand.

Suddenly, Alice grabbed one of the colored pencils and launched herself at Jessica, screaming. She buried the pencil in Jessica's left eye. Alice pulled out the pencil, which now had collected a fair amount of tissue. She slammed the pencil into Jessica's throat. The pencil broke in Alice's hand. She picked up another and shoved it down into Jessica's screaming mouth. Not stopping until she felt something puncture.

Alarms sounded throughout the facility. The orderly grabbed Alice's middle and tried to pull her off. Alice kept yelling words that made no sense when strung together.

Someone called 911. An ambulance arrived within minutes.

"What the fuck happened here?" a medic asked.

"I don't know," the orderly responded. "Alice just started screaming like a banshee and started stabbing with a pencil."

"This damage was all from a pencil?" The medic surveyed Jessica on the ground weeping from one eye and trying to stuff the other back into her head. "Holy shit."

"Yeah. Holy shit."

Chapter Fifty-one

Detective Morrison

Morrison responded to the chaotic scene, taking in everything at once. He saw Alice Smith rocking back and forth, hugging herself. She was covered in blood. An orderly was trying to talk to her. He looked over and heard Jessica Allen screaming while paramedics tried to render aid. He walked over there.

He held up his badge to the first orderly he found. "I'm Detective Morrison. How can I help?"

"Help?" the orderly asked.

"With the situation? This craziness that's going on here?"

"Sorry. I'm not used to police officers asking to help. I figured you just wanted to talk about this mess."

"I understand. I get that a lot. Yeah, if I can help, I would like to. I will need to talk to everyone, but right now, it looks like you could use an extra pair of hands," Morrison stated.

The orderly nodded, "Thank you. Can you go talk to Miss Alice? We're waiting for a doctor to respond, but she needs help. She isn't responding to us. Maybe a new face will get through to her."

"Pretty sure I'm not a new face, but I will try." Morrison walked over to Alice and sat down on his haunches next to the quietly moaning woman. "Hey, Alice. Do you remember me? I'm Detective Sam Morrison. We met before…at the police station."

Alice continued to rock with her hands over her head.

"Alice. I really need your help. What happened here? Do you know?"

More rocking.

"Sir, I don't think she's going to talk. That one gal was just talking to her. We have a video if you want to see it. No audio, though," the same orderly interrupted.

Morrison sighed, "Let me see it."

"The other gal is on her way to the hospital finally. She was not in a good way. Alice has always been calm. I don't know what happened," the orderly said.

Morrison sat in a chair to think. He thought about how Jessica Allen was John Smith's assistant. He considered how John had an affair with both Jessica and Natalie. He thought about how Natalie was dead. He thought about the connection to John. John was the center.

"I think I'm beginning to understand what happened. I think I finally am beginning to see it," Morrison said.

He stood up and walked back over to Alice. "Alice, they say Jessica was here talking to you. That she was here for a little while. Please tell me what happened."

Alice continued to rock back and forth and moan.

"Alice, I need to know. Did Jessica do this? Did she do all of this? What did she say to you?"

Alice stopped rocking and looked up into his face. "She did everything. Everything."

"What happened? What did she say? I need you to tell me."

And Alice told him everything.

Chapter Fifty-two

John

ohn loved Alice. He loved her in a way that he had never loved anyone else. He did what he could to take care of her. She needed him in a way that no one else ever did. She wouldn't be able to live without him. The longer they were together, the more she depended on him.

He loved her family's money that made his life easier. He had grown up with nothing. His mother raised him without any help from his father. Every Christmas, John could expect a Christmas card and a twenty-dollar bill, but that was the extent of that relationship.

He had read about Daniel Patrick in a magazine. Patrick's rising empire. Patrick's single daughter, Alice, was conveniently the same age as John. John moved to the Chicago area and figured out a way to meet Alice. When he met her family for the first time and realized she was the odd little duckling, he knew he could join this family. Alice would allow him to protect her and to make decisions for her. In exchange, he would become an heir to a family fortune that rivaled the Rockefellers.

He planned to serve as the go-between Alice and her parents. He would make sure that she had everything that she wanted and needed. In the process, he would have everything that he wanted and needed. It would be a fair exchange. He would trade her emotional worth and desires for money. She came from so much money that giving some to John amounted to giving him a random trinket.

He would never have had an affair. An affair requires an emotional bonding. An investment in a relationship. His investments both financial and emotional were with his wife. He explained that to all of the girls he enjoyed over the years.

Having an affair never occurred to John.

Never.

There were other women, certainly. He was a man, was he not? He would have a tryst, a dalliance, with a young lady every now and then. Generally, he would throw these women away like used tissues. Who cares? What type of woman would sleep with a married man and expect any type of commitment?

A woman not deserving of a commitment.

He liked being in complete control of these relationships. Their psyches dependent on him. He would play with them. Maybe, sometimes he went a little too far. He understood that. It wasn't his fault. Women just made it too easy. Too fun.

When Jessie came into his life, he should have known. He should have acted quicker. He never suspected that she had that amount of darkness in her. That amount of need.

When she had stabbed him the first time, he was too shocked to reach out. To try and stop her. She hadn't seemed so different from any one of the other "arrangement" girls.

John supposed a man had to be wrong in his life sometimes. It was unfortunate that his mistake cost him his life.

As he lay there in his own blood after Jessie had left, he worried about Alice. Would she be able to navigate this world without him? She was so fragile. So delicate. He hoped people would see that, but not prey on her. Not everyone would understand the fair exchange of wealth required to protect Alice.

John hoped, also, that he would live long enough to see her again.

He did not.

Acknowledgments

First, I want to thank everyone who has taken the time to read my novel. It's something that I've wanted to do for a very long time. I only just sat down to write it last year. I appreciate so much that people have actually read it and (hopefully) enjoyed it.

Next up, I would be remiss to not thank my husband. For someone who doesn't like to read, he has been a champ and read numerous edits of this manuscript. I wouldn't be here without him.

I'm so happy that so many people lined up to help me edit and to read it through. Thank you to my alpha readers who took the time to read it and offer constructive feedback. Thank you to my beta readers who told me how much they enjoyed it. I want to especially acknowledge Coral Mitchell for taking the time to do a thorough edit. Thank you!

My last and final thank you is to those establishments who let me sit for hours and drink tea and write (Here's looking at you BookNook Café). I appreciate so much that you gave me time without trying to rush me along my way.

Don't miss another exciting novel by
Kristine Elizabeth Wolfe!

Fallen Star – Available on Kindle Vella

When the tranquil voyage of a luxury cruise ship is shattered by a mysterious power outage, the passengers and crew find themselves sailing into a storm of chaos and uncertainty. Among them is Gary, an Iraq war veteran, whose past battles have prepared him for the unexpected. Haley, a nurse, and her Nana work to provide comfort to fellow passengers. Throughout it all, a third group forms challenging the fabric of their survival. Will they be able to find a way home?

Thank you for reading my novel! If you enjoyed it, please follow me at any of these platforms to find out when my next novel is debuting!

My website -
www.kristinewolfe.com

LinkedIn page -
https://www.linkedin.com/in/kristinewolfeauthor/

Medium account -
https://medium.com/@kristinewolfeauthor

Please sign up on my website to receive my newsletter!